Presented to

_____

On the occasion of

_____

From

_____

Date

_____

JERRY B. JENKINS

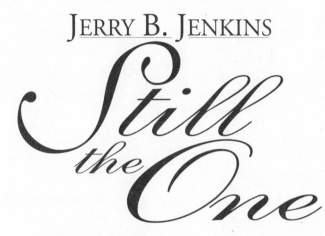

Still the One

Tender Thoughts from a Loving Spouse

Colorado Springs, Colorado

STILL THE ONE
Copyright © 1995 by Jerry B. Jenkins. All rights reserved. International copyright secured.
The author is represented by the literary agency of Alive Communications, P.O. Box 49068, Colorado
Springs, CO 80949.

Library of Congress Cataloging-in-Publication Data
Jenkins, Jerry B.
    Still the one : tender thoughts from a loving spouse / Jerry B. Jenkins.
       p. cm.
    ISBN 1-56179-339-6
    1. Marriage—Religious aspects—Christianity.   2. Love—Religious aspects—
Christianity.   3. Jenkins, Jerry B.—Marriage.   I. Title.
BV835.J47   1994
248.8'44—dc20   94-23328
                                                        CIP
Published by Focus on the Family Publishing, Colorado Springs, CO 80995. Distributed in the U. S. A.
and Canada by Word Books, Dallas, Texas.

Editor: Larry K. Weeden
Cover design: Brad Lind and Alan Cox
Photography: Tim O'Hare

Printed in the United States of America
95 96 97 98 99/10 9 8 7 6 5 4 3 2 1

Contents

1.   Dearly Beloved . . .   1

2.   Who Gives This Woman . . . ?   13

3.   I Take Thee . . .   25

4.   To Be My Lawfully Wedded . . .   37

5.   To Love, Honor, and Cherish . . .   49

6.   In Sickness and in Health . . .   61

7.   For Richer, for Poorer . . .   73

8.   For Better or for Worse . . .   85

9.   For as Long as We Both Shall Live . . .   97

10. With This Ring, I Thee Wed . . .   109

11. You May Kiss . . .   123

12. I Now Present Mr. and Mrs. . . .   135

     Notes   147

Dearly Beloved...

A few months before we married, I looked at your childhood photographs in a well-worn album and was overcome by a strange emotion. I saw you frolicking with your siblings and cousins in clothes and near cars that dated such pictures. I imagined myself during those years and realized with deep feeling that I loved you even then, long before we had met.

When I daydreamed of a lifelong mate and hoped for a relationship such as my parents had, my young heart was filled with love—toward whom?

1

When I read love stories and imagined myself married, who was the object of my budding adoration?

When I dated and learned to interact with the opposite sex and thought about a future with someone to love, about whom was I thinking?

It was you. I didn't even know you, but it had been you all along.

When the minister began our wedding ceremony with those two words, "Dearly beloved," I was transported. How many weddings had I attended, and how many times had I heard those same words, signaling me to tune out the rote ceremony? I would come back to consciousness in time to notice the darling flower girl or the cute ring bearer, wince at the quivery voice of the bridegroom, or smile at the rehearsed yet awkward kiss.

But this time, when it was our own wedding, I would not block out anything. Perhaps in the bustle of wedding plans we should have thought of a less-traditional opening, just to keep people's attention. Yet we had not, and now, with those two words, we were off and running headlong into an adventure, a lifetime journey without map or compass.

The rehearsal had been a most emotional time for me, uncharacteristic nervousness overcoming me in front of only those dearly beloved who would participate with us in the ceremony. How would I function before a sanctuary full of those who cared about us?

The minister had not rehearsed his "Dearly beloved" that night, so it hit me fresh on the big day. *Dearly beloved,* I thought. *That's you. You are the most dearly beloved on earth to me.* And yet he was addressing everyone. Our grandparents, our parents, our brothers and sisters, our best friends, our old friends, our new friends, our temporary friends, some who seemed dear to us at the time but whom we would never see again.

That "Dearly beloved" encompassed even those who were not with us that day. There were those we wished could be there. We each had a grandparent who had "gone on before," as our forebears so delicately put it. How we longed for them to share our joy and excitement, and how deeply we finally understood their legacy! Decades gone, their values—their heritage—lived on through our parents and ultimately through us.

I never knew the grandfather who died when my own father was an infant. Yet down through the decades came evidence of his faith, his devotion, his commitment to God. My brother was his namesake, my father—to hear others tell it—the embodiment of his soul. Years hence, I would repeat the words to the great song "Does Jesus Care?"

3

to our own son as he left for college. Only later would an elderly aunt tell me that that very song was sung at my grandfather's funeral nearly a quarter century before I was born.

You barely remember the grandfather who died when you were a child, and yet his wife was with us on our special day. His twinkle and love of life remain in her and their descendants. Many must have been thinking of him when the minister said, "Dearly beloved, we are gathered here in the presence of God and these witnesses . . ." He would have so loved to have been one of those gathered to see his eldest grandchild take such a momentous step.

Nervous, excited, flush with love, I wanted to not let the archaic language, the ceremonial nature of it all, reduce this to mere formality. I confess some weddings I had attended had that impression on me, while bride and bridegroom seemed to drink everything in as if it were new and unused.

Now I understood. When it's you, you and your dearly beloved, who embark on this oft-reported and yet always unique passage, everything is repainted in vivid colors. As familiar sounding as are the vows and charges and pronouncements, they take on a meaning all too real and ominous when they're being said to, and by, you. I can never claim to remember every word, every detail, every hue. But I do recall opening myself and welcoming all that could fit to sear itself onto the memory banks of my mind and heart.

Moments before the "Dearly beloved," I stood peeking into the sanctuary while friends teased that I had but seconds to change my mind. There would be no changing of this mind, however, and not simply because of the many people who had driven long distances to be with us. I would not be panicking, would have no hesitation, no second thoughts—at least not today. I was nervous, yes. Laden with the ominous gravity and seriousness of it all, of course. But these dearly beloved were gathered with me and my dearly beloved for the touchstone event of our lives. I had never been so sure of a decision in my life.

Childhood friends were there. Friends from lifetimes in church. Friends we hung with in high school and college. In-laws, a niece, a nephew, aunts, uncles, cousins. How quaint to refer to them all as dearly beloved, and yet on this day it became clear that they were. In much the same way that we realize at Christmas how treasured are our friends and family, this day we were moved by those who had honored us by accepting our invitation.

Some may have been there out of obligation or tradition. More important than their reason for attending was the mere fact that they were there. In their diverse ways, they had shaped our lives. We were, and thus our union would be, a product of their collective input.

Many were known only to you, others only to me. We would introduce them to each other at the reception and explain briefly the impact they had had on our lives.

As independent and self-made as I might have been tempted to feel that day, it was that church full of dearly beloved who made me realize what a derivative I am of those who surround me. Some influenced me positively, others negatively. Yet I couldn't argue that the diversity of influences there had affected the choices I had made. And as it has been so eloquently stated by others, our lives are not measured by the things we accomplish but by the choices we make.

Many of the dearly beloved who were with us that day are no longer alive. Yet their influence on us remains as strong as that of those grandfathers who had gone on even before our wedding. The storytelling, the acts of kindness, the selflessness, the unbridled laughter—these did not die with our loved ones. They are reproduced in our alliance and in our children.

How can I forget the seemingly minor and yet to me nearly unspeakable kindness once offered by a person who sat in the sanctuary that day? A few years before, he and I had been traveling with a sports team and had stopped for dinner. Each was to pay for his own meal. When I realized I had not brought enough cash, I whispered a request to him for a couple of dollars.

How easy it would have been for him to make an issue of it, to make a joke at my expense, or to be public about his generosity! Yet he knew instinctively that this was an embarrassing moment and that even the asking had been difficult. I had been nearly overcome when he slipped me the money under the table so no one else would know.

How many others there that day had influenced our young lives in much more profound ways? I saw aunts and uncles and cousins with whom I had spent countless holidays. Just to know there were other families who shared my parents' values was life shaping. I had been scolded, corrected, and treated like one of their own. Painful as those moments were, it was comforting to know they cared enough to want me to grow up properly. That made it all the more meaningful when they exulted in my achievements and triumphs, and when they chose to share my joy that day.

I also met some of your people on our wedding day, ones I had seen only in pictures. With each name had come a story, and I slowly began to feel as if I knew them all through you.

We had both been influenced by the others in our childhood photographs. There were those in that sanctuary after whom we would not want to pattern our lives. Yet still they were dear and beloved.

We were learning to accept know-it-alls, skeptics, grumps, critics, mockers, and the snooty. They helped us with examples of how not to function with others. Loving them in spite of their quirks would make us mature and, we hoped, aware of our own foibles. Gradually, we would learn what kind of friends we wanted to be or not to be, what kind of husband and wife, aunt and uncle, mother and father, grandmother and grandfather—all from those dearly beloved gathered together that day in the presence of God and other witnesses.

During the opening music, as I surveyed the faces, I knew it would be so easy to let the hour slip past with an eye on the clock, worrying about the choreography, the formalities, the receiving line, the reception, the gifts, the cake, the getaway, the honeymoon.

A relative had joked, "All the bride and bridegroom need to know is how to get the tux on and the dress off!" There were times when that seemed a freeing thought: Stick to the basics, concentrate on the fun and excitement. Yet we couldn't; we must not let this ceremony become merely a prerequisite.

An elderly saint embraced me in the foyer before the service and whispered in my ear, "May your lifetime of marriage be as beautiful as the hour of your wedding."

I smiled and thanked her, but the sentiment didn't register until I stood scanning the beloved. Yes, of course, the marriage was infinitely longer and more important than the wedding. Beautiful as the ceremony was, it would make little difference if someone forgot a cue or a line, if someone fainted, if something fell. And hadn't we all seen gorgeous, expensive weddings that seemed to last longer than the contentious marriage?

But the woman had not denigrated the importance of the wedding itself. She merely wished that our life together would always be as beautiful as this exhilarating day. She knew as well as we did—maybe more than we did—that it would not be so. No one can or should maintain that level of an emotional high for days on end, let alone years.

Yet her point was well taken. And if the marriage was to forever bear the imprimatur of friends, family, the church, the Father, and Christ, it behooved me to understand it. I've been in churches where the worship service itself is made up of rote recitations. Yet even there, when I forced myself to stop and listen, I found the sentiments rich and deep with beautiful meaning. The words were not without significance; the people had lost touch with the point due to constant repetition.

What I noticed most about the dearly beloved that made them even more dear and more loved were their smiles and their tears. They were truly sharing with us the emotion, the joy and the melancholy, of the moment. Our parents sensed—better than we did at the time—the significance of the stepping stone this was, the new chapter in our lives and theirs.

There could be no more denying it. There was leaving and cleaving happening here.

Others, relatives and friends who had known us in various ways, may have been hearing us express love to each other in solemn terms for the first time. There was wonder on their faces. This was no longer adolescent rhapsodizing about someone's looks or personality. This was a commitment of love and faithfulness forever, a bonding of flesh and soul ordained by God and superseding all other proclamations we had made.

There were a few in the church, of course, whom we might not have described as dear or beloved, but in the ensuing years, the mere fact that they shared that most sacred event with us has endeared them—or their memories—to us. For whatever reason or motive, they were there, and they have become part of our collective memory.

A greeting-card sentiment talks about today being the first day of the rest of your life. If ever there was a special day to embody that thought, it was the day of our wedding. Momentous days would follow: discovering we would have a child and all the significant rites of passage for him and the two who followed—kindergarten, salvation, puberty, baptism, learning to drive, leaving home. But for us, just the two of us, this was our day, our launching. This was, indeed, the first day of the rest of our life together.

Among the dearly beloved that day were middle-aged and older couples, some who sat together but whose body language showed they merely coexisted. Had they not once shared the same joy, anticipation, and dreams we now had? What had become of their young love? They scared us. They had become more like shirtsleeve relatives to each other.

Others, married for decades, still shared a touch, an embrace, a smile. Their treatment of each other showed they had not lost their first love for one another but rather had nourished it and seen it grow into a mature, deep relationship.

That was what we wanted. That was what we determined to cultivate. We wanted the dearly beloved to always remember that they had been with us on this day when something so momentous had begun.

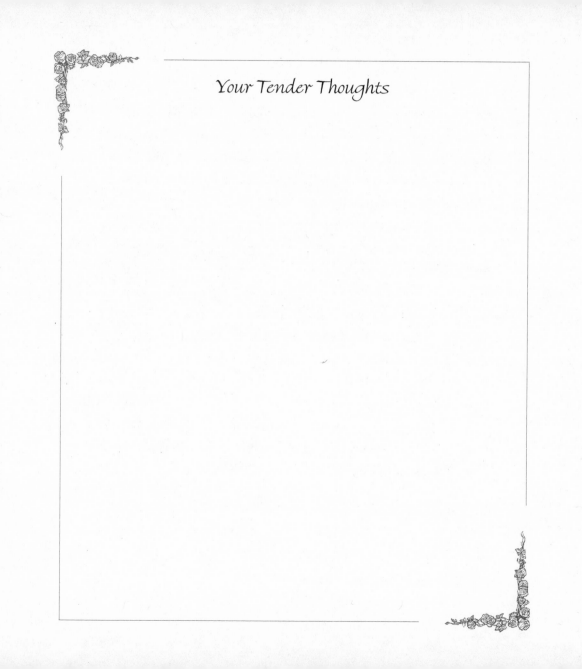

Your Tender Thoughts

Who Gives
This Woman...?

*I*f ever there was a portion of a Christian rite that would set a feminist's teeth on edge, it's this phrase. Indeed, most of secular society deems archaic, even barbaric, the notion that a woman is a possession, a thing to be given, bartered, or traded. Yet in some cultures today, young women must still be purchased by their bridegrooms. A friend of ours from another country had to put off his wedding for a year because he couldn't afford the price his future father-in-law asked for his daughter: cash and a goat.

Yet in our case, we didn't view this phrase or this part of the ceremony as demeaning to the bride. She was still her own person. This union was her decision. She had not been coerced or pressured, except gently by her own dearly beloved, of course. Her family had not pushed the idea, at least not the timing of it.

Her parents gave their blessing but wondered with bemusement, "What's the rush?"

We countered with a smile, "If you don't know what the rush is, you have poor memories!"

Yes, we admit it. We were eager to consummate our love. We were not marrying early to accommodate a pregnancy. We would not bear children for nearly five years. Now, after two-plus decades together, we understand the perspective of physical love in the broad spectrum of married life. What seemed so important on our wedding night has taken its proper place in the whirlwind of daily life. We may even try to counsel our children that while what seems paramount now will still be beautiful, exciting, fun, rewarding, and important later, it will not occupy center stage after a while. But they won't be listening. This is something that must be learned, not taught.

All that to say that no one was pressuring the bride; no one was telling her whom to marry or when. No side deals were made; nothing

14

was arranged or stipulated. Truly, nothing was done without her input and veto power. She was asked. She had the option. She said yes.

Rather than shrink from the idea that her father, on behalf of him and her mother, had the right to "give this woman," she believed that rite of passage esteemed her parents most of all. There was honor in the giving. It was a symbolic gesture.

Until she left the nest, she submitted to her parents' authority. Their ownership was not of her being, of her mind, or of her soul. It was of her well-being.

In our culture, she did not have to wait for their blessing, their giving. Had such figurative, voluntary permission been withheld, she could have done as so many others have. She could have proceeded on her own. And perhaps she would have been right, depending on the legitimacy of the reasons for her parents' disapproval.

Such a voluntary giving of life's most precious gift is no small thing, something that became crystal clear to us when we had our own children. They never seem old enough for whatever passage has arrived in their lives.

Perhaps it does seem sexist and demeaning for only the bride to be given. Is not the bridegroom being released as well? While we don't customarily express this in the marriage rite, surely someone is giving "this man" as well. A welcome addition to the close of the ceremony is the modern custom of bride and bridegroom honoring both sets of parents with embraces and flowers.

It's only right that the support and sacrifice, the nurturing and rearing, of both sets of parents be honored. They never claimed to be perfect, and perhaps their parenting was wrought with error. Still, the ceremonial "giving away" of the bride, though brief and preliminary, is a crucial part of the pageant. It is not the work the parents did so much as the people themselves and their intent that are recognized. Despite their humanness and shortcomings, parents and their roles during the formative years should never be ignored or diminished.

Nevertheless, marriage is a time of redirection, of pursuing a new path that involves leaving. This also moves us up one rung on the generational ladder. Bride and bridegroom are no longer children but will likely become parents themselves. Now is the time to learn from parents' mistakes and incorporate their successes as the couple forge their own life's values.

Because we both grew up in evangelical Christian, churchgoing families, we share values and memories despite not knowing each other until we were in our twenties. We both know what it means to be in church twice on Sunday and once in the middle of the week.

We've been to countless potluck dinners and buffets, family reunions, and church picnics.

Fascinating in all these memories is to see the relentless march of time and what it does to the roles of individuals. I can remember a childhood of sitting at the little kids' table, cavorting in the other room while the adults talked, and playing tag in the churchyard. At family gatherings, my cousins and siblings played for hours.

It wasn't long before we were going through puberty together, becoming awkward, self-conscious, gangly. Our older cousins were falling in love, going steady, getting engaged and married, and we watched in fascination as they introduced their new loves to the family. Class rings were traded, diamonds were presented, announcements were made. Kids whose voices had changed just a year or so before were now driving, sitting close to each other, looking longingly into each other's eyes.

Before long, we attended their weddings. They seemed so mature and adult to us adolescents. But now, with the perspective of time, we know how young and raw they were. Soon their babies were the ones in the bassinets and then in the playroom as we moved up a notch or two on the ladder of progression.

Back then it seemed time passed slowly, but nothing would seem slow again. People we remember as merely older cousins are now parents. Don't blink. They're now in their late forties and even early fifties. They're grandparents. Their kids, those babies and toddlers who chased us into adolescence, are parents themselves.

Life marches on. Roles change. Who gives this woman? Whole families do. Histories, legacies, customs, heritages, generations. We go from being children to being part of the "older set" so quickly we are stunned. When these babies grow up and begin looking like their parents, our minds reel.

How young must the bride have appeared to her parents on our wedding day! Indeed, a month before our own wedding, we attended the twenty-fifth anniversary of my parents' union. Now we're middle-aged, not two years from our own silver anniversary and probably not five from grandparenthood ourselves.

Who gives this woman? It must have seemed to the father of the bride that he wasn't so much giving as seeing her slip through his fingers in the inexorable passage of time.

Only as parents have we realized the depth of emotion, caring, and love our own parents must have felt for us. We had no clue before. Parents were just there. To some they are burdens, frightening, someone to overcome or rebel against. For us, we merely had to mature to learn what a wonderful endowment we enjoyed. What might have frustrated us about our parents years ago we now try to emulate.

The strictness and rigidity we once resented we now try to duplicate. Sure, there are things we do differently and—we hope—better. But when we hear our kids complain about teachers, coaches, and superiors who seem unbending and strict and have too-high expectations, we privately applaud. That's the type of molders of character we want for our kids, because that's the way we were raised.

Though the father of the bride is speaking for both himself and his wife when he says, "Her mother and I do [give this woman]," because he alone walks her down the aisle and makes the response, many ascribe to this moment particular pain for the man. In truth, there *is* a unique bond between a father and a daughter, and this can become evident as early as the first time his precious toddler is joined in the sandbox by a preschool boy.

He may pace and look out the window, spying, keeping track, ever vigilant. He may even mosey out, pretending to do something else while keeping watch. What's he afraid of? The sad truth is, he has too good a memory. He may not remember precisely when sexual thoughts first entered his mind, but he can't remember when they weren't there, either. He fights the urge to ask a kid with pail and shovel, "Just what are your intentions, young man?"

When she does begin to date, it's always way too early—at least in Daddy's eyes. His wife might have to remind him how young she was when she first dated. Is it possible his little girl is the age his wife was when he met her? Please, no.

And when the real dating has begun, the father feels—rightfully so—that he does now have the right and the responsibility to set the record straight with the young man. It's fair to know who the boy is, who his people are, what he drives, how he drives it, what his reputation is, where they'll go, what they will and won't do there, and when they'll be back.

A friend, the father of two daughters, admits he doesn't mind putting a little fear into the boys. His daughters may be embarrassed when he asks for a few moments alone with their dates, and he might rather the young men think he's an okay guy than that he's a mean, protective father. But some things are worth a little awkwardness. Boys might think such dads are a little overprotective. To the fathers of daughters, however, there is no such thing as overprotective.

Another friend says he uses a sports-car analogy to get his point across. He'll say to the boy, "If I owned the most expensive, exotic sports car on the road and I let you take it for a spin, you'd be careful with it, wouldn't you?"

"Oh, yes, sir, you bet."

"You'd treat it better than if it was your own, wouldn't you?"

"Yes, sir."

"I wouldn't want to think you were screeching the tires, would I?"

"No, sir."

"Well, let me tell you something, just so we're straight with each other, man to man. My daughter is of infinitely more value to me than any car could ever be. Do you get my drift? She's on loan from me to you for the next few hours, and I wouldn't want to discover that she was treated with any less care or respect than I would give her. I'm responsible for her. She's mine. I'm entrusting her to you. That trust brooks no second chances. Understand?"

By then, of course, the young man is wondering why he didn't ask someone else out. He's only nodding, unable to speak. Most often, he brings the girl home earlier than promised. The daughter might even complain about her father's approach, but down deep she feels loved and cherished, and you can be sure she'll marry a man who treats her that way.

The big interview with the father used to come only when the young man was ready to formally ask for her hand in marriage.

Someone has said that there's only one appropriate answer to "Are you prepared to support a family?"

It's this: "No, sir, I'm not. I'm prepared to support her; the rest of you will have to fend for yourselves."

Seriously, though, I appreciate the legendary story of Grant Teaff, former head football coach at Baylor University in Texas. He made sure he was the first man to date his daughter. He waited until she was of dating age and had been asked out by someone. She knew she had to ask her parents' permission, and when she asked, he told her to put the boy off for a week. Meanwhile, he himself would take her out.

He called her, formally, from his office and asked if she was available and interested in going to dinner with him. When she said yes, he told her where they would be going, what would be appropriate attire, when he would pick her up, and when he would deliver her home.

At the prearranged time, he arrived, came to the door, waited for her, greeted her, complimented her, opened doors for her, talked to her, listened to her, treated her with deference and respect, and followed through with all the plans he had told her about. He was charming and funny but never offensive or improper. At the end of the evening, he took her home, walked her to the door, thanked her, and made sure she got inside before "leaving."

Afterward, there was a debriefing. She was reminded that he had not slid up to the curb late and honked his horn, expecting her to run out. She was reminded that he was cordial to her and to her mother, and that he had treated her like a queen the whole night.

Then he looked her in the eye and told her that that's what she deserved. Sure, a date might just be for fun and getting acquainted. Few first dates result in a serious relationship, let alone marriage. Still, he expected her to be treated like a lady, and he urged her to accept no less.

What he knew, of course, was that every date she had after that would be compared to her first with him. Whoever eventually won her heart would have to treat her at least as well as had her own father, the one who brought her into the world.

Who gives this woman to be married to this man? On behalf of him and his wife, he's simply another man, an older man. A farmer, a police chief, an executive, a truck driver. He might be shy. He might be gregarious. Whoever he is, he will be painfully removing himself from the life of one of the most important loved ones he has ever known. To him it may feel as if she has been excised surgically from his very heart.

It won't be easy. He simply prays it will be right.

Your Tender Thoughts

I Take Thee...

These are merely the first three words in a sentence repeated in some form in almost every wedding, yet each word is a universe unto itself.

I. Who am I? I'm the product of all the years I've lived, the family and friends who have influenced me, the teachers who have mentored me, even the detractors who have taught me. I'm a product of every school and church I've attended, every sermon and speech I've heard, every book and article I've read.

More important, though, who do I think I am? Who am I to take anyone, let alone you—the object of my desire—to be my lawfully wedded spouse?

Take. I'm taking you. You're taking me. The choice of a lifetime mate is second in importance only to our decision to receive Christ as Savior. How ironic that this most important, most complex choice usually comes at an age when we're least qualified to make it! At the same time, we're young enough to believe we know it all. With little or no experience and none of the wisdom of age, we are cocksure of ourselves, led by our passions and our hearts, and so we sail confidently into uncharted seas.

Knowing that God intended this taking of each other to be an exclusive, once-for-all decision, we are not deterred. Somehow that makes us surer than ever in our hearts that we have each found the right person, the one of God's own choosing.

Only after we've been married a while do we wonder at our youth and naïveté. How did we make that choice, that decision? Was it luck, coincidence? Did we really allow God into the process? Did we tell ourselves what we wanted to hear? Believe what we wanted to believe? Were we guilty of what songwriter Paul Simon said in his famous tune "The Boxer" about a man hearing what he wants to hear and disregarding the rest?

I happen to be a romantic, a nostalgic, melancholy type who believes there is one man and woman meant for each other and that God delights in ordering our steps so we find each other. Smarter, wiser, more educated people than I would call that blather. Even spiritual leaders I respect greatly say there are probably any number of candidates with whom we could enjoy satisfying marital unions, and any one of them might be in God's permissible or even perfect will.

Yet I prefer to believe that our courses are traceable. I look back on where I was, whom I knew, and where I was going when our paths crossed for the first time. I don't even want to consider that we weren't destined for each other. On the other hand, that kind of thinking can be damning for someone who is merely trying to justify marrying the wrong person. If it seemed like a divine coincidence, a surprisingly opened door, he or she might decide God has to be in it, true or not.

Those kinds of emotional decisions can have disastrous results. An old joke tells of the bride who stopped halfway down the aisle and sang, "I'd Rather Have Jesus." Worse are the true stories of seemingly star-crossed couples who realize on their honeymoons, or shortly thereafter, that they've made a terrible mistake.

What a tragedy to discover that your loved one has fallen out of love with you, doubts his or her original decision, or feels trapped in a marriage already regretted and repulsive! Those of us who believe marriage is God's idea and who believe that even mistakes—if they were made before God and sealed in heaven—should not be torn asunder feel deeply for people who feel trapped in such relationships. It's of little consolation to them to hear that they must make the best of it, must make it work in spite of the loss of sparks. People don't want to hear that if they act in a loving manner, the feeling of love will return. What they need to know from the beginning is that love is as love does. Love is not a state of being, it's an act of the will. It's not something you're in. It's something you do.

Sure, the warm fuzzies are more fun. That rush, that pounding heart, that need to be together—those are pleasurable, life-making feelings. But when they fade, true love must take over. True love is an action verb. It's expressed by doing, by preferring one another over ourselves. And dark as that tunnel may appear when someone decides early that a dire mistake has been made, love *can* be rekindled, and feelings can and will return.

Those, however, were the kinds of fears and misgivings I had when we decided to marry. It wasn't that I expected to have second thoughts; rather, in my own insecurity, I feared against fear that you would come to your senses. How could someone so wonderful find me attractive and appealing enough to marry?

To marry. That sounds so easy. We went through a brief ceremony, and we were married. But to marry means to join with, to become one with, to pledge a lifetime of exclusive love and support. How could I qualify for that? It was like the old joke: "I wouldn't want to be in a club that would allow me to be a member." To me, your only shortcoming was in your choice of a spouse: *moi.*

I am influenced by my faith, indwelt by my God, shaped by sermons and lessons and lectures and modeling. I've been molded by friends and experiences unique to me, and I've tried to react against intrusions that might have made me less than you deserve.

My greatest fear is also the source of my greatest joy: that I'm not worthy of you. And yet you chose me. How Christlike you are in that! Of course I'm not worthy of His love, forgiveness, and acceptance. No one is. And though I know marriage is intended to be a picture of the wedding of Christ and His church, I didn't expect the analogy to go this far: that I would experience on a human level that love and acceptance that can be described only as divine.

Thee. Now, there's one of those Elizabethan or King-James-English words that young people smirk at. Certainly it's an example of the stuffy language that makes marriage rites and vows so easy to ignore. Do they really mean anything; do we take them seriously? Every day, people are bailing out of marriage as if they had made no promises, no commitments, and had done nothing sacred, moral, or legal.

Yet everyone knows what *thee* means. It means "you." And who are you? I hardly know who *I* am after a lifetime. I continue to be amazed that I was given the privilege to "take" you—especially as I learn over the years that the you who is you is forever changing.

You're also a product of influences, bringing to our home a rich tapestry whose detail I can appreciate fully only as the years reveal it.

When I think of you, I rotate your name in my head, fascinated that in one name is contained your essence. You who are so many people and personalities wrapped into one are identified by a first name that has become as commonplace as breathing to me because I use it dozens of times every day. When I talk to you or about you, your name rolls unconsciously off my lips. When I think about it, allow myself to hear the sound and cadence of it, it becomes almost foreign, strange sounding. How can one name carry so much meaning?

I easily remember that one of my first impressions of you had to do with the sound of your voice. Now I have to force myself to listen to see why it was so engaging. I'm so used to it now, I would be startled only if it changed. Just as we've grown used to the smell of our house surrounded by pungent pine trees—to the point that we don't notice it until visitors point it out—I've grown accustomed to your voice.

Some say your voice is difficult to hear in a crowded, noisy room, not because it's so soft but because it's so low. We joke that to be heard you must raise it an octave and speak nasally, which you choose not to do (gratefully). But that deep, throaty richness in your voice is part of your essence to me. Maybe I read too much into this, but to me the richness of your voice speaks of your character. Perhaps there are those with deep voices who are shallow in character. With you that is not so.

In one compact frame, one that you are disciplined and caring enough to maintain, reside all the many elements that make you uniquely you.

You see, I thought I knew what I was getting when I married you. I didn't have a clue. The longer we're together, the more I learn and the more I realize I don't know. That makes my life an adventure of discovery. Best of all, and underscoring my theory that we were destined for each other, is that every new vista I discover is more amazing and pleasing.

How dreadful it would have been to discover that I had been duped, that you had sold me a bill of goods, that you were not what you appeared to be. I had high hopes. We were both young and blinded by love, but I was sure I detected more than physical attractiveness. There was something there, someone I could grow old with, someone whose mind, spirit, personality, and character would keep my interest.

How thrilled I am that I was right! I'm not saying you're perfect any more than I am. Though in our courtship I suspected you might be flawless, I was warned enough by counselors and mentors to get that crazy idea out of my head. People who think they've married perfection often come to crushing reality in devastating ways. When they discover that their loved one is human, earthy, and blunt, and that he or she can be irritable, selfish, illogical, or frustrating, they nearly self-destruct.

I confess I'm pleased to find that I'm much more irritable, selfish, and so on than you are. But either way, I could endure reality. Why? Because at your core, you knew yourself. You knew who you were and never claimed to be anyone or anything different.

It was a surprise to discover that you were as awed by my love for you as I was by yours for me. That was more than a surprise, really.

More of a shock. I was so in love that I thought anyone—even you—could see that it was logical for me to love you. To discover that you—like me—had some deep-seated insecurities was stunning. And such are not all bad. As I thought about that, I realized that if you had an inkling that you were worthy of the depth of love my heart generates for you, you would be impossible to live with. As long as your insecurities don't handicap you, don't turn you into a bitter, self-loathing person, a small dose of their reality makes you humble.

What more attractive quality can a wonderful person have? We both know wonderful people who know they're wonderful, and suddenly that makes them less wonderful. You've never been comfortable being worshiped (while I wouldn't mind giving the idea a try). Yet to have been able to convince you over the years that at least I think you're wonderful has been a remarkable accomplishment.

I thought I knew you when we were both young, but by the time I really thought I had you figured out, you had lived more years. You had interacted with more people, learned more things, made more decisions, become a parent. (How fun it was to see you go from being a laid-back, soft-spoken, almost shy person to becoming a protective authority figure!)

Within a few years, you had read your Bible more, prayed more, studied more, listened more. You had taken in more of the education life had to offer. In many ways you were the same person you had always been, with the same core, the same personality, the same character. On the other hand, you had processed so much more of life that you had nearly become another person. I'm grateful that the new person is one I admire and love, and at times I wonder what might have become of me—of us—if you had changed for the worse.

I also wonder if you can say I've changed as well and whether, if you can, the current me is either what you expected or a major disappointment, compared to the early edition.

As Christians, we want to grow in the likeness of Christ. That's my highest goal and most nagging frustration. The more I learn about Him, despite whatever growing I'm doing, the further I seem to fall short. There seems to be no end to His beauty and majesty, which ironically makes even a growing Christian seem smaller all the time.

What gives me hope is that I've seen you grow spiritually. You're living proof that it can be done. You would pooh-pooh the notion of being considered "an example for the believers" (as the apostle Paul said), but again, that's what makes you who you are. Had you shrunk spiritually, become lukewarm or inconsistent, I might have wondered if I were the cause. Spiritual growth isn't easy, and when I see once-on-fire couples drifting from their passion for Christ, it makes me long for us to be to each other whatever we need to be to keep us accountable.

I take thee. I take you. It was the best decision I ever made, better even than I knew or dreamed it could be. To think that you feel even a fraction the same about your decision to take me makes my loftiest dream come true.

Though embodied in one person, one body, one mind, one countenance, your universe of experience, thought, and personality is bestowed on the one blessed enough to share your life with you. It's a priceless treasure I will never tire of mining.

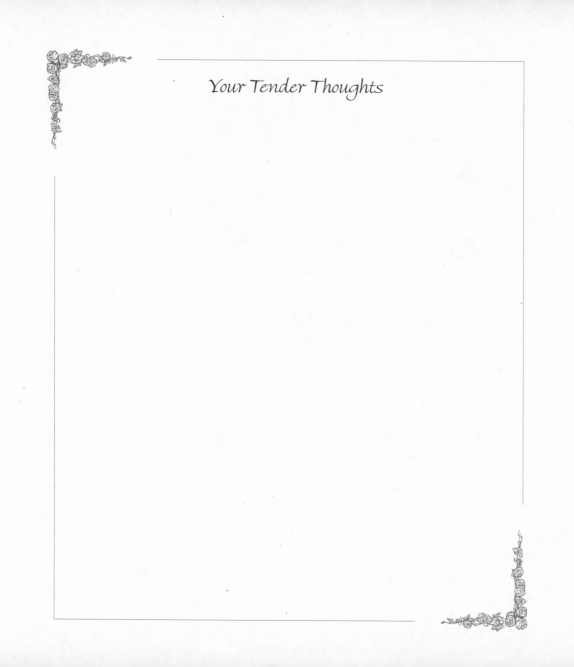

Your Tender Thoughts

To Be My
Lawfully Wedded...

The operative word in this phrase is, of course, *lawfully.* Of all the phrases and words we used and heard the day of our wedding, *lawfully* may have been the one that most easily slipped past us. It was so obvious, so understated, so nearly redundant.

While divorce was not part of our vocabulary and never will be, neither were adultery, fornication, shacking up, living together, or common-law marriage.

Sure, people were doing it back then—living together outside of marriage, I mean. That idea has been around forever, of course, but it became popular in the late sixties, rampant in the seventies, and is by now commonplace. Huge numbers of couples live together with nearly all the rights and privileges and many of the responsibilities of marriage, but without being lawfully wedded.

Just about every day, you can see examples of such couples on any one of several TV talk shows. Not long ago, our own high-school student reported that one of his teachers had announced that she and her fiancé had moved in together and would likely be married within the year.

No one seems to blink at this anymore. We knew, of course, that such an arrangement was one of many options for an in-love couple, even 20-plus years ago in the dark ages. But it was not something we considered. We didn't even think about it. We would be lawfully wedded because that was the right thing to do.

An old adage says that stolen sweets are sweeter. Another says there is nothing so passionate as an illicit love affair, with the possibility of being caught at any time. I am so thankful to say that I have no experience with stolen love or illicit affairs. I was a virgin who married a virgin, and that is a treasure above all others, something that could never be sold, bought, or traded.

I sincerely doubt that whatever thrill comes with a guilt-producing liaison—and I'm not doubting that such might be of pleasure for a while—could hold a candle to a lifetime of sexual fidelity. We are lawfully wedded. And we shall be lawfully wedded for as long as we live.

There's peace of mind in that. There's comfort and an easy meshing of the gears of our minds. With clear consciences we enjoy each other, probing the depths of each other's being more every year. We know each other inside and out. We know what the other is thinking and feeling. We can read a look, a raised brow, a tone of voice. We know when the other is smiling and yet merely tolerating a boor. We can be conversing with a group and maintaining a private conversation on another level, all at the same time.

We know each other's weaknesses, and we don't exploit them. We know our idiosyncrasies. While some people trade in their spouses for hot new models every few years and substitute overt sexiness for communication, we really know each other. When in public you surreptitiously stab off my plate what I consider a repulsive food item (so I don't have to be embarrassed at leaving it), you display an easy knowledge of me born of years of clear-conscience cohabiting. When I cover for you in awkward situations or we finish each other's sentences, we're coordinating as one in the business of life.

There's nothing so freeing or comfortable as the process of becoming one. That doesn't mean we don't have minds of our own, that we're not distinct beings in ourselves. It does mean that we've chosen to become students of each other, majoring in each other.

I can't imagine starting over with someone else. I'm no more tempted to take up with a younger person than I am to rob a bank. Oh, I understand the appeal of indulging in an affair. After years of marriage, it's not uncommon for people to see and even be attracted to someone who seems younger, fresher, more alive than their spouse. Such an affair might have briefly pleasurable aspects. But it would be wrong. I wouldn't be able to live with myself. There's no substitute for enjoying what is truly, legally yours. We have grown comfortable with each other. That doesn't mean we take each other for granted. It means that we know, we understand, and we anticipate needs.

I find myself talking about you when you're not around. Long ago we discussed how unattractive it was to hear spouses bad-mouth each other. Heaven knows it would be easy to do. Find some quirk, some irritating habit, and make a joke of it. But that's not love. Love is building up each other. If ever someone tells you he or she heard me talking about you, that person will have to say I was praising you. It's all I do.

We've both known couples who make their own laws so that in their own minds they remain "lawfully wedded." Dear friends of ours believed they could be intimate before they married because they were in love and had pledged their exclusivity. Soon after they married, however, they decided that an open relationship was the best and most honest. In other words, they could still date and even sleep with others as long as they were candid about it. Their consciences may have been salved for a while with their telling each other everything. But that's not my idea of lawful marriage. They are—no surprise here—now divorced.

Open marriages don't work and rarely last, because that's not what God intended. One partner gets caught roaming, insists to the other that openness was what he or she was really after, and then caves in to jealousy and remorse when the other partner calls his or her bluff and accepts the generous offer of reciprocity.

In my mind, lawful weddedness means more than just a slip of paper. People can be legally married by a justice of the peace. But is their union legal in the sight of God? Have they made Him a partner in their relationship? Is their goal that the marriage itself become a testimony to Christ?

When the minister tells the dearly beloved that they are gathered together "in the sight of God and in the face of this company," there's a reason. Marriage was God's idea. That's why it's called holy matrimony.

I confess we had been married many years and had attended several weddings before the gravity and seriousness of it all hit me. You know I've been committed to faithfulness and to our being lawfully wedded, but countless repetitions of the ministers' charges at various weddings really drove it home for me.

The typical pronouncement is that marriage, or holy matrimony, is "an honorable estate, instituted by God, signifying unto us the mystical union between God and His church; which holy estate Christ adorned and beautified with His presence and first miracle that He wrought in Cana of Galilee, and is commended of Saint Paul to be honorable among all men: and therefore is not by any to be entered into unadvisedly, but soberly, and in the fear of God."

That ought to be enough to scare some people off.

Then, in quick succession, the officiating minister presents scenarios that would render the wedding, the marriage, unlawful. First, to the assembled he says, "Into this holy estate these two persons present come now to be joined. If any can show just cause why they may not be lawfully joined together, let them now speak, or else hereafter hold their peace."

In other words, say it now or shut up about it. Bring a charge and
have it dealt with, or never bring it up again. This is always a tense,
awkward moment in a ceremony, often eliciting embarrassed grins.
Yet who hasn't wondered if someone might leap to his or her feet
with a claim that either party had already been unfaithful? Or that
one of them had promised love to another? What a nightmare!

I've heard stories, perhaps apocryphal, of someone standing to
claim a previous promise from the bride and the minister needing to
publicly ask the wish of the parties. In the story—or legend—I
heard, the betrothed reaffirmed her pledge to the bridegroom, where-
upon the minister charged the interrupter to accept her decision and
from that point on hold his peace. Of course, the bringer of the
charge then retreated in remorse and humiliation.

Another story (also likely legendary) tells of a bride answering the
minister's question, speaking up at this explosive moment of tension
to say that she saw her bridegroom *in flagrante delicto* with her own
maid of honor the night before. Such urban legends are told and
retold because they carry such irony. The poor bride was betrayed not
only by her intended, but also by her best friend. And then her
revenge was presumably sweet, exposing them to the world at the

worst possible moment before leaving them at the altar.

Of course, there are many holes in a story like that. One can hardly imagine a person so wounded and betrayed that she would have the wherewithal to pull off such a vengeful act. Yet the odds are that somewhere, at some time, such a scene has been played out. If the gossipmongers can be believed, Princess Diana knew enough to have been able to embarrass her prince on their wedding day. If true, what a charade that beautiful ceremony becomes!

The officiating minister then addresses the couple themselves. He says, "I require and charge you both, as you will answer at the dreadful day of judgment when the secrets of all hearts shall be disclosed [you can see why it is little wonder that many modern ceremonies have omitted this phraseology and, indeed, the whole idea of anyone telling what they know], that if either of you know any impediment, why you may not be lawfully joined together in matrimony, you do now confess it. For be you well assured, that if any persons are joined together otherwise than as God's Word doth allow, their marriage is not lawful."

Many couples consider this part of the ceremony particularly dreadful and negative and delete it. And yet, in this age when God's laws are so blithely disregarded, a pure couple should revel in the opportunity to stand tall in the face of such dire warnings.

Is the bride or the bridegroom a liar? Has either been sexually impure? Has either pledged his or her love or hand to another without setting the matter straight before marrying? This is not to say that either party, having sinned with another before marrying, should be forever banned from marriage. You'll recall that our minister, who also served as best man, began our pre-wedding private consultation with the straightforward question, "Are you pregnant?"

We were stunned but pleased to tell him no. I was curious. I asked what he would have done or said if we were, indeed, expecting. "I would have wanted to make sure you had repented of your sin [of premarital sex] and also that you didn't feel a hasty marriage would make a problem disappear."

This is not to be taken lightly, but clearly the God who sent His Son to die for our sins can forgive sexual sin and will not forever disqualify a person from enjoying marriage. To be lawfully wedded, however, a couple must have all such sin confessed, repented of, and put under the blood of Christ. In other words, past sin must remain past sin.

We all know of couples who are hastily married—white dress, big church wedding, and all—who have just discovered they are two or

three months along in a pregnancy. Such news travels so fast that
they fool no one in either family and thus no one attending the wedding. Their every move and statement, and especially their wedding
kiss, is scrutinized for inappropriateness and gall.

The poor bride. Because she's usually young and pregnant for the
first time, she may not be showing yet, but you can bet every eye is
looking for signs. Are such couples being lawfully wed? Only if
they've confessed and repented. Are they obligated to publicly confess? That would not be for me to say, certainly.

Should they be allowed the big, festive wedding and the virginal
colors, or are those merely traditions? That's for the couple and their
counselors to determine. If they choose to project a false picture,
however, the early delivery of their child will reveal the truth to the
world.

Many such rushed marriages work, of course. Some are sad cases
where neither party had been promiscuous before. In the heat of passion, they made a mistake with the only person they had ever loved.
They had planned to be married anyway, and they moved the date up
to protect the child from a lifetime of tongue-wagging.

These are always tragic cases, because even God's people have trouble
forgetting sordid details. Decades after such marriages, someone is

bound to let slip that "you know so-and-so [referring to the couple's son or daughter] was the reason they got married when they did."

Sad but true, we cannot forget the sins that God says He will separate from us as far as the east is from the west.

The idea, of course, is a wedding lawful both in the eyes of the state and in the eyes of God. Such is one of the great treasures of our life.

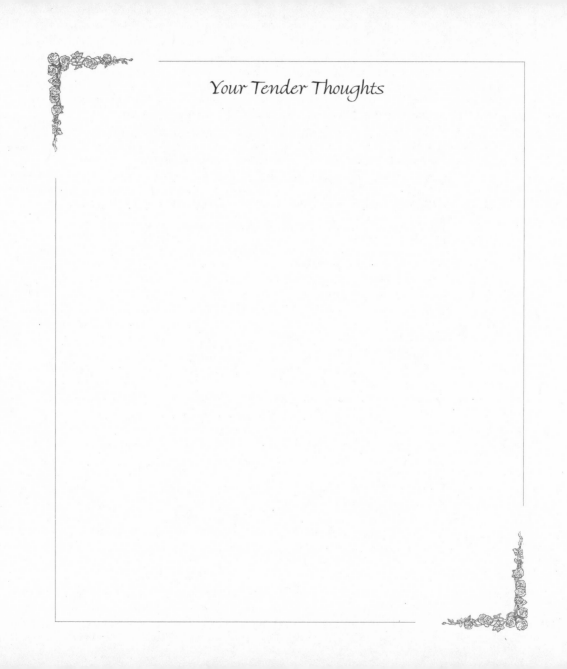

Your Tender Thoughts

To Love, Honor, and Cherish...

Clearly, loving, honoring, and cherishing are foundation stones of a solid marriage. Further, when we see these evident in a relationship, they reflect our worth as God's unique creations. My goal is to generously shower them upon you daily to strengthen the bond that will last a lifetime.

Loving, honoring, and cherishing are more than ideals, more than concepts, more than words or feelings. They are actions best exercised in the daily grind of life. And while it's true that actions speak louder than words, I want always to remember that oral and written expressions of love, commitment, and esteem are also imperative. How I long for and appreciate the same from you!

Sometimes these words—*love, honor,* and *cherish*—run together so quickly in their recitation that they seem indistinguishable. Yet they're distinct in themselves.

Love. As I said earlier, love means action. To merely say you love someone rings hollow after a while, especially if no actions back it up. In much the same way that faith without works is dead,[1] so expressions of love without the grit of proof are empty.

How often have we seen abusive, alcoholic, or unfaithful spouses cry, beg forgiveness, and pledge their undying love? "Why should you forgive me? Why should you come back to me? Why should you let me come back to you? Why should you believe me? Because I've proved my faithfulness and fidelity and sobriety? No. Because I love you, love you, love you." Sadly, many victimized spouses fall for this rhetoric every time.

One of the most fundamental adages of the writing game is "Don't tell me, show me." When writing fiction, it's one thing to say, "She was mad." It's quite another to write, "She flung the pen across the room, walked out, and slammed the door." Show, don't tell.

That's also good advice for those who want to express their love.

Lest I be misunderstood, I must say that many marriage partners live and die to *hear* the words "I love you" from their spouses. When they go for weeks or months hearing no such expression, they sometimes can't hold back any longer. They burst forth with, "Don't you love me? Can't you tell me? Can't you say it?"

Then the closest they get to an "I love you" is, "How can you say that? Of course I do. I married you, didn't I?"

That's usually the signal that the case is closed. But if the wounded spouse can't let it drop and still expresses the need to hear the words, the offender might further defend, "Aren't I always there for you? Can't you tell? Aren't I kind, generous, and faithful?"

There's a lot of truth to that. Still, we need to hear the words. For people who didn't hear expressions of love in their childhoods, it's difficult to say that phrase. It may roll easily off their lips during courtship, but when they've already won the hearts of their desired ones and life settles into routine, they slip back into old habits.

That's why it's important to make saying "I love you" a habit. Sure, there's a danger it may become rote and lose its meaning. But the benefits of being able to say it without embarrassment are worth the risk. When the chips are down and your spouse needs to hear it, you can say it without hesitation. You can also sense when he or she needs a dose of verbal encouragement like that.

Again, however, if your actions haven't given the words any meaning, it's better not to speak emptiness. Someone is treated dreadfully for weeks, then hears his or her spouse say, "You know I love you," and wishes nothing had been said. It would have been more honest, the offended person feels, to have said the opposite. "I hate you" makes more sense and more accurately reflects what has been going on.

Something about saying "I love you" when you mean it makes you want to prove it. One of the most treasured elements of my heritage is the love relationship between my parents. What made it special was that in talking with them individually, I came to believe that they both felt genuinely unworthy of the other. What a loving, giving relationship resulted from that! They proved their love for each other every day in myriad ways.

They knew how to express their love conventionally: the right gift, the right word, the right written sentiment on the appropriate special day. But they also knew how to show tenderness and compassion, friendship and familiarity. Dad could have just risen, be sitting in the kitchen barely awake, unshaven, hair independent of control, yet Mom would greet him with a hug, a kiss, and a kind word.

Draping a blanket over a napping partner is a thoughtful gesture of love. Removing eyeglasses from the face and a book from the chest of a dozing spouse is a sign of affection. He or she wakes up and recalls having fallen asleep mid-chapter, and there are his or her glasses and book on the bedside.

Love is knowing the other's order at a restaurant if he or she is away when the waiter arrives. Love is occasionally doing your spouse's least-favorite chore. It's not a big deal. Neither may mention the event. Such displays become part of the fabric of everyday life.

Don't just tell me, show me. And don't just show me, tell me. And whatever you do, don't tell me and then show me otherwise.

Honor. Honoring is a little different, but, of course, it ties in to love. We sometimes honor people we don't necessarily love. But how much more meaningful—and easy—it is to honor the one we love the most in the world.

I intend to honor you when others generalize negatively about spouses. I enjoy saying, "That's not universally true. That's not true of my spouse." People call their spouses their "old lady" or their "old man." She might refer to him as "big and ugly"; he may call her his "ball and chain." You'll never hear that from me.

Honoring means proudly introducing you in every social situation, taking and showing pride that you're with me. Honoring means talking positively about you when you're not with me. I don't mean being obnoxious and boring people with lovey-dovey tales of my royal partner. But I'm always prepared with a good word about you, because it comes naturally.

Honoring also means putting the other ahead of yourself. It's amazing how easy it is to do the opposite. We're such selfish, self-obsessed creatures. I dash to the kitchen for a couple of pieces of fruit, one for you and one for me. One slips and rolls across the floor. Which do I give you?

The answer is obvious. I love you. We've been married for years. We're familiar with each other. I've already won your heart, and you wouldn't know the difference if I gave you the more-well-traveled apple. The shame is that the temptation remains to put myself first. (I'm happy to say I ate the bruised one.)

Honoring means deferring to each other, too. That can be a trap. If one spouse is a whiner, a complainer, a pouter, demanding and childish, deferring could better be described as keeping the peace, catering to the person, enabling, or promoting such behavior. I'm glad I haven't had to work through that in our relationship.

Obviously, it would be better for the more mature spouse to help engender some emotional growth and not to merely acquiesce in order to avoid a scene.

In our case, it's fun to see that we've both learned to give. Sometimes even this can be frustrating. We spend a lot of time saying, "No, really, whatever you want. You decide. I'll be happy if you're happy." I happen to be one who applies the biblical model of the husband as head of the home solely in situations of major conflict, when we're truly at loggerheads. Otherwise, it seems the best solution is to prefer one another, submit to one another, honor one another.

An elderly man is reported to have said that he and his wife enjoyed 50 years of wedded bliss because he made all the major decisions and let her make all the minor decisions. He explained that in five decades, there had been no major decisions.

It's unbecoming to see a couple—usually the husband, of course—take the head-of-the-home responsibility to the point where he feels he must win every argument. The family goes where he wants to go, does what he wants to do, eats what he wants to eat, and does everything at the time he wants to do it. They buy the home he wants, redecorate the room he wants redecorated in the color he chooses. If he and his wife disagree on something they saw on TV, she's expected to submit to his authority—as if authority means he has a better memory and better ideas.

While I hate to generalize, I do believe that most men—if they're honest—admit that their wives are wiser than they are in many areas. Doesn't a mother know better when a child is tired and cranky and needs to go to bed, no matter what Dad thinks at the time? If a wife suggests that the youngster not stay up for another game, the husband should submit to her motherly instincts. It's no sacrifice of authority.

This authority question should rather be seen as a heavy spiritual responsibility, not as license to have the entire marriage and household revolve around the man—what kind of loving, honoring, and cherishing is that?

Cherish. Now there's a quaint, romantic word that doesn't get enough use in our society. Is it merely a redundancy after loving and honoring? I think not. It is, however, dessert to the loving and honoring's meat and potatoes. Imagine how you'd feel if I didn't really love you—by showing it or saying it—and neglected to honor you, yet I adored you, worshiped you, mooned over you, lavished gifts upon you, spoke in the most reverential terms about you.

Gag!

Wouldn't that make you ill? Would I exude any personal power, presence, or strength? Anyone would love to be worshiped once in a while. A compliment, a bit of adoration, can make your day. Mark Twain said he could go two months on a good compliment.

But being cherished all the time would be like eating only strawberry shortcake. The third or fourth in a row would begin to get old. (Okay, maybe the fifth or sixth in a row.)

In my mind, cherishing is for special moments. Cherishing a spouse is similar to the feeling you get when you bend over a sleeping newborn and study her tiny fingers in a sliver of light from the window. The room is dark. You have played with the infant, fed her, changed her, bathed her, hugged her, kissed her, caressed her, talked to her, sung to her, rocked her, and put her to bed. Now you come back and cherish her.

I cherish you when you weep at an emotional moment. I cherish you when you show divine selflessness to someone else. I cherish you when you're funny, when you're embarrassed, when you're sad. Your emotions bring out my emotions, and those emotions are often accompanied by cherishing.

An old song says *cherish* describes all the feelings we have deep inside. Again, it's emotion based. We love our kids. We honor our friends. But we cherish our grandparents and the memories of them.

We love our fine collectibles. We feel honored to have heirloom dishes. We cherish mementos of past Christmases. When our tree toppled over this Christmas and we lost half a dozen ornaments, we were less affected by the smashing of a couple of fairly expensive glass pieces than we were by the shattering of cheap, little papier-mâché symbols of our kids and their childhoods. We loved the expensive ornaments, but we cherished the meaning and memories embodied in the handmade ones.

Cherishing is often an unstated thing. Some people might sound natural saying, "I cherish you." I reckon I wouldn't and that it would sound strange to you. I might write it, and you know it's true. It's simply a different issue, a deeper, more contemplative emotion. When the Scripture says that Mary thought back on all the events of the nativity of Jesus and pondered them in her heart,[2] I suspect she was cherishing the memories.

I want to love you the way Christ loved the church and was willing to give up His life for it. That's an ideal, and my greatest fear is that if put to the test I would panic and think of my own hide first. Yet I find myself drawn to love songs, love poetry, and love expressions in cards, and the object of my love is you.

I want to honor you every day, preferring you over myself. That, too, goes against my pedestrian grain. I'm a selfish creature, and sometimes I think that in loving and honoring you, I'm doing the same to myself, because you're a part of me. We are one. But if honoring and loving means putting you first, then there's always the striving to keep pure motives. I want to act out of a pure heart, not giving in order to get, doing to get a response, acting merely to be noticed or appreciated.

Rather, I want to do all this to prove my love, to truly honor you, and to cherish you the way you deserve.

The best part of loving, honoring, and cherishing you is that you're truly convinced you're unworthy of it. That's what makes these feelings so much more rewarding and easy to entertain. Sad to say, in too many marriages, the partners no longer have—and perhaps never had—this feeling of unworthiness of the love of the other. That's impossible to fake, and its absence from a marriage is a tragedy.

As was true of the way my parents felt about each other, however, I don't feel worthy of you, either. Your true humility makes you only more special to me. May it ever be so.

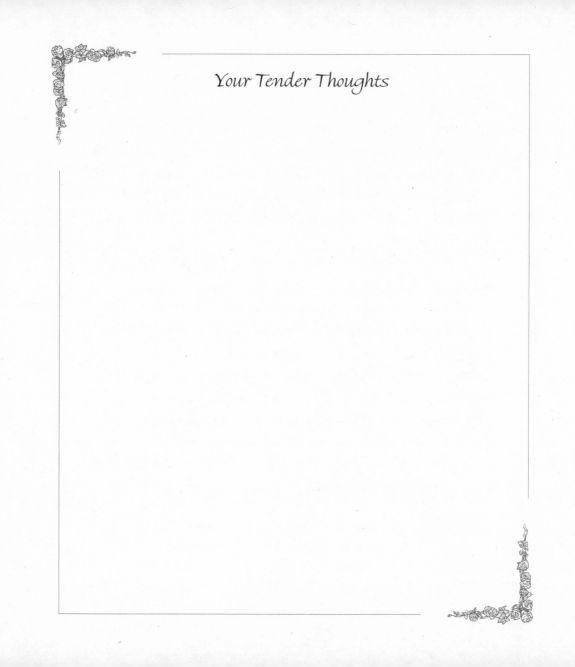

Your Tender Thoughts

In Sickness and in Health...

True love survives even apart from youth and energy; it prospers in the trenches amidst pain and heartache. As surely as the sun rises and sets, so health fades. Though sickness intrudes to destroy plans and alter priorities, its challenge can also help us discover the truest, deepest meaning of love.

I wish you no ill, no sickness, no sadness, no heartache. I would protect you from every evil if it were in my power. There were fleeting moments in my youth when my love was so unbounded and naive that I thought I did, indeed, have that power, merely because of the depth of my feeling. Age teaches hard lessons. My love has not diminished, yet I now know that protecting you against every evil is beyond my control.

Knowing we face trouble as surely as the sparks fly upward, I will not plot one step of retreat or escape. When the day comes that I'm called upon to prove the true depth of my love by remaining constant in my devotion—whether because of some ailment or tragedy neither of us would wish on an enemy—I will embrace that season as a privilege. I love you not merely for your beauty and your health, but also for who you are inside.

If the worst happens and you lose even the knowledge of what's going on around you, still I will support you, love you, honor you, cherish you, and take care of you, fulfilling my vows with joy in spite of agony. No one would be thankful for that eventuality, but I believe I'll be able to be thankful *in* that circumstance, God forbid, because my adoration for you is deep.

As I am committed to being your stretcher bearer if and when necessary, pray that I'll be willing to graciously accept you as mine should I ever become physically or mentally dependent. Sometimes I think that would be worse. No sane, healthy person wants to become totally dependent. That can result in bitterness and negativity. The incapacitated can become demanding despite his or her hatred of the loss of independence.

To write about standing by you in times of sickness is particularly strange due to your unusual history of healthfulness. In more than two decades of marriage, you've been bedridden only one full day. You've never been hospitalized for sickness and treated only a few times for the occasional injury.

We joke that you come from good Midwestern, country stock, yet it's no joke. You have little patience with minor ailments. There's no hypochondria in this family. Were we a football team, we'd be known for playing hurt. The truth is, your friends are probably right when they insist that perhaps you should have spent more days in bed, recuperating from colds, the flu, or migraines. Yet you've always been one who wants to get on with life. If you're incapacitated, okay, you'll take a brief break. But as soon as you start feeling better, you're back in action.

You've always been an early-to-bed-early-to-rise person. I'm amused at how it's as if someone has pulled your plug around 9 o'clock every night. (Others, of course, are exactly the opposite, just coming alive at 9:00 P.M.) Then the vivacious person who has been going 100 miles an hour since sunup—even during sedentary pursuits—shuts down and could sleep standing. I can't say this has made you healthy, wealthy, and wise—as Ben Franklin opined—but two out of three ain't bad.

Your vigor and health make strange this writing about your eventual demise. Though every living creature is destined to run down and die one day, the odds are with you. You will likely outlive me simply because you're healthier, more fit, less ground down by various ailments. I've come late to the fitness and nutrition game, and while I enjoy it and feel as healthy as I've ever been, you seem to have had a knack for conditioning all your life.

I remember early in our marriage when you didn't work out as religiously as you do now. And though you probably weren't as careful about nutrition as we are today, still you were always vigilant. It has been years now since you began working out hard five days a week, and you're a constant inspiration to me. You don't nag. You don't have to. You just lead by example. You're going to work out whether I do or not, so if I don't want to compound my laziness by feeling worse, I must simply get at it.

All that to say that I can't imagine my hovering over you in the winter of your life, fulfilling the vow embodied in this chapter.

Would it surprise me if you were struck down by some ailment? If you grew old and infirm before your time and mine? You bet it would. But I don't want to be naive. Just because I can't picture it doesn't mean it can't or won't happen. The belief that bad things happen only to others gets all kinds of people in all kinds of trouble—like teens who think they can't get pregnant, daredevils who think they'll live forever, and criminals who "know" they'll never be caught.

I'm well aware that we have an adversary and that he seeks to kill, rob, and destroy. You don't feel like it, but the fact is, you'd be a prize for the evil one. He'd love to do you in, because he would be affecting all those you touch—particularly our immediate family. Our children are being molded into strong, active Christians largely because of you. They're principled and disciplined (or they eventually will be—honest).

Hear me: I'm not predicting anything dire. I'm not a pessimist. I just want to make clear that I'm realistic and pledge that I'll be here for you if and when you need me to be, regardless.

It doesn't seem that long ago that I didn't even have to consider this. In fact, the day of our wedding, I certainly wasn't thinking about old age, senility, disease, or misfortune when I promised to love you in sickness and in health. I probably thought of a common cold—which you rarely get.

You were so young, so fit, so healthy, so alive. You still are, yet we've both seen people our age and even a bit younger suffer through untold turmoil. Loved ones have died—grandparents, aunts, uncles, even dear friends. The Scriptures say life is but a vapor that appears for an instant and then vanishes away.[1] Sadly, we learn the truth of that more clearly with every passing year.

Somehow, in our minds, we feel no older than we did when we met. When nothing excited me more than your arrival from out of state, we felt the world was before us—the world and unlimited time. Now, though we feel no older, the mirror doesn't lie. The aches and pains don't lie. The calendar doesn't lie. We're headed the way of all flesh, so we must rethink and renew this vow.

I'm moved when I hear stories of love that stands the test of such maladies. I remember early in our marriage when we visited friends of my parents. They were an elderly couple, and the woman had fallen deathly ill. Her husband, a quiet saint, didn't want her to waste away and die in a hospital, so he brought her home to their tiny apartment. He rented a hospital bed, and he nursed her 24 hours a day.

I felt guilty sitting there, trying to be cordial, watching her die.

Conversation was awkward, at least from us. He basically tended to her: got water and medicine for her; fed her; moved her; talked to her. When she was comfortable (she was past conversing), he would turn to us and smile and talk about her. He would bring us up to date on her condition, whispering when he got to the dire prognosis and the woefully short life span now predicted.

We asked if he ever got a break, and he assured us that she slept sometimes three hours at a time, especially during the night. We deduced that he was otherwise basically on call. People from the church asked if they could relieve him, but he usually declined. If he did accede to a lunch date, he continually looked at his watch and was uncomfortable until he could get back to her. He sensed she was restless without him there.

We asked what he did for diversion, and his answer nearly broke me. He hauled out his spiral notebooks full of prayer lists. "You're in here," he said. I was stunned. We had never met. He had heard of us only through my parents, and yet there we were, listed by name. On a certain day of the week, he prayed for the offspring of his friends. He had page after page of prayer lists from friends, relatives, friends of friends, relatives of friends, missionaries, the country, the world.

"I don't see *you* on these lists," I said.

"I'm so blessed," he said simply, taking his wife's hand.

She would die within a matter of months. The way he talked about her—what a wonderful companion she had been and what a special mother to their children—it was clear that there was nothing he would rather do in the world than take care of her in her hour of need.

Clearly, he would rather that she was healthy. He hurt for her. It was frustrating. But he took this hand he was dealt, and he played it for all it was worth. He embraced the tragedy and counted it an honor to give himself to her, to invest himself in her comfort. He wasn't merely keeping a stiff upper lip. He was joyful, glad to do it, honored.

Oh, if I could be half that devoted if and when the time comes!

My own grandfather had a difficult job for the last several years of my grandmother's life. (I can say this now that they're both gone.) Disease had taken its toll on her body and her mind, and thus her spirit. She had been a vibrant woman of faith for most of her life, but then her myriad physical ailments began to take their toll. She was unable to get around by herself and lost her vision and hearing, and she became demanding. Those who visited their home told stories of hearing her call out to him repeatedly. "Dale!" she would cry in the night, waking him.

Without complaint, he would go to her and help her to the bathroom, get her something to drink, or merely soothe her. He was loving the girl he married, not the troubled woman she had become. He was old and not entirely healthy himself, yet he never complained. It had to be difficult to be on constant alert, even while dozing after a long day of thankless service. He tried to keep himself occupied with hobbies, but even those finally had to take a backseat to her constant care.

Yet he never bad-mouthed her. Everything I ever heard him say about her was loving. Admittedly, most of it was memories of better days, but that was what he dwelt on.

She spent her last few days in the hospital, incoherent. She thought she had something in her hand and insisted that he take it. When he told her that her hand was empty, she kept thrusting it toward him, demanding he take it. Only when he pantomimed reaching into her palm and removing it was she satisfied.

"What's your name, little boy?" she would ask suddenly.

"There's no one here, Mom," Grandpa would say. (He always called her that.)

"Have the boy tell me his name!"

"There's no one here but you and me, Mom," Grandpa would say.

"Are you Berwyn or Billy?" she would persist, wondering if the little boy she imagined in the room was her long-since-deceased old-est son or her youngest son, now a grandfather himself.

My grandfather told these stories of her hallucinations with respectful, bemused love.

When she finally passed away, I stood with him by her casket. He was weeping, not sobbing. He was up to greeting everyone and accepting their condolences. But tears ran as he chatted, even as he smiled at this or that memory.

I didn't know what to say, but I knew he wanted to talk about her. "She was quite a woman," I offered.

"She was," he said simply. "We were married in 1917."

I nodded.

"You know, the other day I heard her calling 'Dale' in the night. The funny thing was," he said, his moist eyes smiling, "I got up, got my robe on, and went to her bed before I realized she wasn't there."

In fact, she hadn't been home for quite a while, having died after some time in the hospital. I bit my lip and shook my head. It was understandable that Grandpa wasn't yet used to Grandma's being gone.

"Well," I said in my youth and naïveté, "that part of it has to be a relief to you—getting a break from the constant pressure, being able to get a whole night's sleep."

He shrugged, something he rarely did. "Oh, not really," he said. "I wish she'd have been there. I wish she was still there."

And I knew he meant he would rather have her alive, even in the difficult state she was in, than to have her gone.

I want to fulfill my vow to you like that, my love. No matter what happens to you, I will love you till I die. Even if you die first.

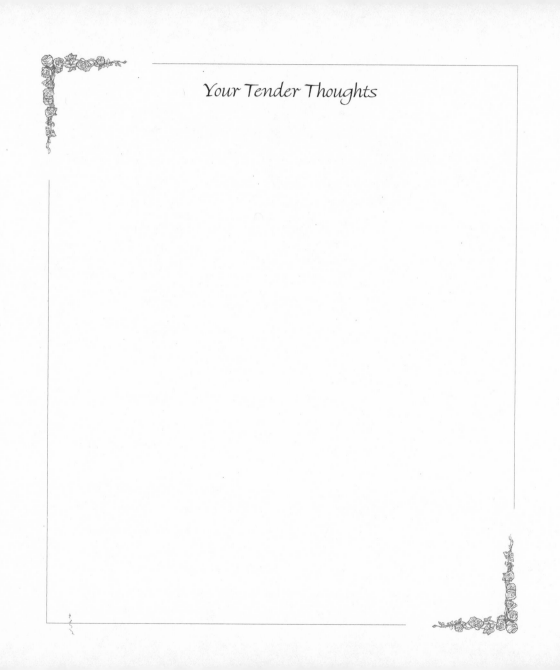

Your Tender Thoughts

For Richer,
for Poorer...

We can easily become the ugliest of material creatures,
harried human beings in search of financial riches. Yet
Jesus Himself said that our lives do not consist of what we own.
Would that we could learn to simplify!

Love in its truest sense is a humble thing. It doesn't depend on
Wedgwood or Waterford; it exults in earthenware. It relishes bare
feet, faded jeans, simple pleasures. Look at the example of the King
of kings Himself. Given the power of heaven and the choice of any

venue in which to enter humankind, God chose not a palace but a stable, not a royal family but a carpenter's, not robes but swaddling clothes.

I want to strive to make your life rich in what really counts, and though we've been blessed beyond measure with earthly pleasures, I pray generosity will be our hallmark.

Like most couples during the period we were married, we started meagerly. Compared to how it had been for our parents a quarter century before, we were way ahead of the game, however. And admittedly, even in our era there were those occasional young people who started with a home, a honeymoon on some island, a new car, and enough wedding gifts and cash to carry them for months.

But for normal people like us, it was an exciting, difficult adventure. Much as I want to avoid clichés, I have to admit that we have never been happier than we were in those early, struggling days.

I used to joke that while our friends were honeymooning in Acapulco, we were enjoying the South Bend-Mishawaka weekend package. In truth, we didn't get that close to Indiana. We spent our honeymoon night in Peoria, just north of the farm community where our wedding had been held. Our honeymoon consisted of driving across the country to the state of Washington for my new job.

We knew two people in the state, and we had to find an apartment, locate the newspaper office where I would work, buy enough sundries and groceries to set up housekeeping, and, after you grew bored in a few days, find you a job as well.

What a time we had, getting to know each other! We would be married four months before we knew one another a full year. We realized marrying so quickly was a risk, but ours was no star-crossed, whirlwind love affair. Well, maybe it was, but we had also been careful, studying each other, learning about each other, seeking counsel and input, being sure we weren't moving too fast.

We would panic today if one of our kids met someone and married that hastily. It makes no sense; it's against all odds. That it has worked out so perfectly for us is miraculous. I've always believed we were meant for each other, but when I see how our personalities mesh, I also think we were very lucky. I would attribute that to God, too, but I know of many, many other Christian couples that I believe belong together and have wonderful marriages, but whose personalities don't connect so smoothly.

So, there we were, basically newlywed strangers in a new city and a new state, 2,000 miles from our people. In reality, it was the best thing that could have happened to our marriage. There was no one to run to, no one to interfere. There were few distractions. We weren't together every minute because of our jobs, but we looked forward to getting back together at the end of every day. We were each other's lifeline, each other's sustenance.

We found a church and became youth sponsors. Can you remember ever having enough spare time to volunteer for something like that?

What simple pleasures we enjoyed! A hoagie from a hole-in-the-wall place was a special, once-a-week treat. A hot fudge sundae after church while reading a fresh copy of the Sunday paper with my weekend sports stories in it was a highlight (at least for me). Going together to the sporting events I covered, visiting your boss's family on special occasions, and driving across the state, through the snowy mountains to Seattle, was like honeymooning again.

We read, watched TV, went to church events, had people over. Meanwhile, I was paying off your engagement ring and making a car payment, and between our two incomes we were able to comfortably handle the rent in our one-bedroom, furnished apartment.

We didn't have much extra cash, but neither did we have extra needs. Our desires were simple, and I have to say, so were our aspirations. We didn't look far ahead. I was doing what I had always

dreamed of doing and living with the most precious person I had
ever met. If I had a dream, it was to one day catch on with the sports
department of a major-market newspaper like the *L.A. Times* or the
Chicago Tribune. If I thought about it, I might have liked to envision
myself as the sports editor some day, maybe when I was an old
codger in my thirties.

What we didn't know when we got to Washington, of course, was
that my new boss, nice and shy and soft-spoken as he was in the
office, was a drunk outside the office. Within a few months he had
lost his job, the little, close-knit sports department became chaotic,
and we got a new boss. He was a great guy, and I was learning a lot
from him, but something happened to me one day. I was reminded
of an important fact.

I had stopped by the post office on my way home from work and
caught a glimpse of myself in the reflection from the window. There I
was in shirt and tie, all of 21 years old and looking like an adult.
Something had been nagging at my subconscious for weeks. Now it
hit me. I had made a commitment, a pledge, a vow, many years
before meeting you. I hadn't actually forgotten it, but somewhere
along the way I had rationalized my way into adjusting it to fit my
needs, goals, and desires.

At age 16, I had gone forward at camp in answer to a call to full-time Christian service. I had felt the Lord speaking to me that night when the speaker talked about the vineyard and how ripe it was and how few laborers there were. He clarified that there was certainly nothing wrong with Christians working secular jobs and shining for their faith in that venue. In fact, he said, many of them would have wider, more effective ministries than some who chose traditional Christian ministries.

And yet, he said, sometimes God calls people to work full-time in His service—make their living, in other words, in ministry. I felt that call and made my commitment.

It didn't bother me that preachers and missionaries were typically underpaid. I was raised in the home of a civil servant, so I knew what it meant to get along and enjoy life without opulence or luxuries.

And yet as I grew older and got into sportswriting, I kept putting off my call. Dreaming about being a big-city sports editor one day had to fit in the category of a Christian trying to live out his faith in a secular environment. It was a lofty and perhaps idealistic and naive goal. And it was also a departure from my commitment.

Seeing that reflection of myself appearing all established and grown-up brought me back to earth. We may have been living the modest life of Riley, but I had also been raised by people of principle. You and I had been playing house and enjoying a wonderfully idyllic early married life of several months. I began getting the urge to grow up even more and start taking some serious responsibility.

There was nothing wrong with how we had started. In fact, as I say, it remains one of the great memories of our life together. And maybe the urgency to get serious was self-generated; perhaps we could have enjoyed that kind of living for another year or so. But once you get the bug, you have to act.

I prayed about what it all meant. Was I to go back to Bible college? Become a missionary? A pastor? How would we live in the meantime? We had decided (foolishly, we now feel) to wait a few years before starting a family, but still I felt tremendous responsibility to take care of you.

You, as always, trusted God, believed in me (and vice versa), and expressed your willingness to go anywhere and do anything we both knew was right. I couldn't shake the feeling that God had gifted me as a journalist, and He seemed to be impressing upon me that there was nothing wrong with serving Him full-time in editorial work.

With your blessing and approval, I began looking for openings in Christian journalism. Less than a year after marrying and heading west, we were wending our way back to the Midwest, where I began a succession of magazine editorial positions that would result in my becoming managing editor of a Christian monthly.

Again, I aspired to nothing else. To be doing what I loved, following my commitment to serve God by doing it, and making a modest living at it besides was more than I ever could have dreamed. We began our family after four and a half years of marriage and moved into our first very-own house.

We tried to live within our means, sometimes getting into the same credit-card traps that most other people do, but quickly seeing the folly of that and working our way out of debt. Something happened to us, though, that would change forever the way we both looked at money.

I hesitate to lay this out as a model, because I don't happen to believe in a prosperity gospel. Nor do I believe God can be bound to do something for us if we do something for Him. All I know from experience, however, is that He honors obedience. He doesn't necessarily bless sacrifice, but He does honor obedience.

Early in my fledgling Christian journalism career, I had my most dramatic encounter with God. While researching my first book, I believe the Lord spoke directly to my heart as specifically as ever in my life and told me that we should increase our giving. You know well that I tried to talk myself out of this craziness by laying out fleeces that served only to prove my lack of faith. God convicted my heart and fulfilled my fleeces cavalierly. After shamefully trying to disobey what I knew to be a specific urging of God, I realized I had to obey.

But we couldn't afford it. We were living modestly on a limited budget, and our various expenses didn't leave us room to give more. The only way I could increase our percentage of giving was to increase our income. I'd like to say I did that on my own initiative, but God did that, too. He took my willingness and spurred others to action.

The very next day after we decided to go ahead and give more, I received three phone calls, each totally independent of the others, asking if I did freelance writing. "I do now," I said.

Looking back at this point on more than 20 years, countless articles, and more than 100 books, we can only marvel. The extra income, clearly, was not intended for our use. With a few exceptions, we haven't lived at the level it would have afforded us. We were getting in order to give, and I believe it's a matter not of virtue or sacrifice or even generosity, but rather of obedience.

It's gratifying to look back, all the way to before that encounter and its result, to the day I pledged that I would love you for richer or for poorer. I can't say we've been required to live poorer. When we had limited funds, we wanted nothing more. When we had more, we still had to learn tough lessons about credit, investing, and materialism. But we know we can live in times of plenty as well as in seasons of want.

My love for you is not based on our prosperity or lack of it, and you've been such an example to me in this area that you could be writing this with much more credibility than I. There have been times when I've been thrilled to give you something I never thought I'd be able to afford, knowing full well that you're just as delighted with a card or a quiet dinner.

The small, personal, meaning-laden gifts are the ones that reach you. Sure, you love a big surprise, and I know you infer love from the gifts I've given over the years. But you've convinced me (and the knowledge has humbled me) that what you want in our marriage is not *things*. You want me to remember the important dates, sure. But what you really want is me—my time, attention, and love.

Of those there is no limit, regardless of our income. And if our situation changes or misfortune enters our home and drastically affects our resources, the most important things—the things money can't buy—won't change. I see earthquake, flood, and fire survivors on television, weeping over the shocking losses of their homes, and I know our immediate reactions would be the same if we lost ours.

But then to hear those heroic people say, "At least we still have each other; we'll just have to start over"—that's when I see models of resilience, of faithfulness and dedication that endure for richer and for poorer.

That's true love.

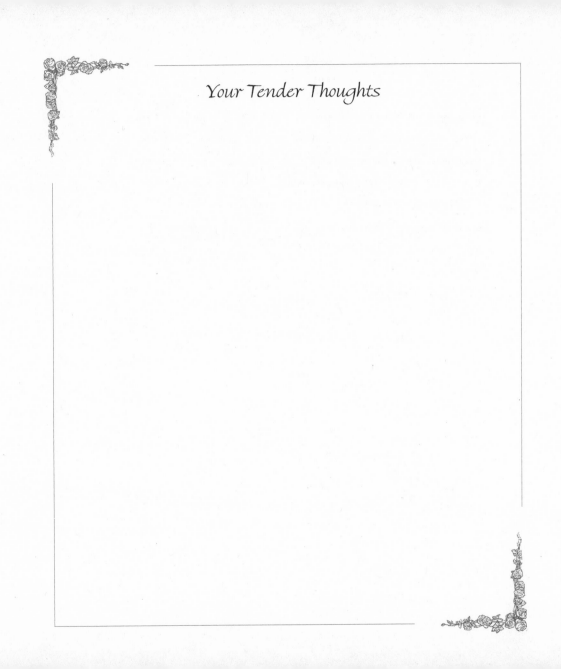

Your Tender Thoughts

For Better
or for Worse...

We've been lucky, you and I. When I consider what most people must endure, I realize we've been most blessed. Even at this writing, however, I'm aware how quickly things can change. Tomorrow may not be like today. Our married life could be a roller coaster of emotion and circumstances—from changing jobs, losing and gaining friends, and even mood swings. My goal is to make our life together an adventure, regardless of eventualities. Through the best and worst of times, as the song says, I'll be there.

One of the hardest lessons for any couple is to learn to cleave tightest—to each other and to God—when it appears the very sun of life has been extinguished. I want always to be an example to you of God's grace and patience. I want to be a reminder to you of the truth that the darkest hour is just before dawn.

What humbles me is that we both made this vow. To know that you'll be with me during the dark times is a great comfort. There have been times when I've felt overcommitted, overworked, overtired, underfunded, and out of time. I needed a good night's sleep before getting even a late start on a project that overwhelmed me—only to find myself tossing and turning, unable to rest.

The more one tries to relax in a situation like that, the more one struggles and suffers. There's a certain desperate loneliness when one is living under those circumstances. Often I keep that kind of pressure from you—foolishly. Whether that's intended to save you the grief or to maintain some illusion of my own independence and immunity to anxiety, I don't know.

But you know me too well, and when you ask, I tell you—not reluctantly but with relief. And you say, "We're in it together. You've done it before; you'll do it again."

You don't do what I do. I'm not sure what kind of spouse I'd be if my mate and I shared the same gifts and talents. Some couples can make that work. It's comfortable for us to have our own specialties and strengths. Yet when you say we're in it together, you mean that psychologically and emotionally, you're with me. You won't be doing my work for me or with me. You might relieve me of some other duty so my schedule will have some flex, but just the knowledge that you're with me allows me to function at my best.

Now married to you half my life, I'm learning the best ways to stand with you. Knowing we're not alone in this complex, changing, scary world makes life such an adventure.

Our first tests came early in our relationship, the very first even before we were married. We had met and fallen in love quickly. We were on a fast track toward marriage when you asked for a week's worth of breathing space. My first reaction was irritation. (It's difficult to be irritated with someone with whom you're head over heels in love.)

I thought you were asking for time and space simply because that was a typical thing your friends did in their relationships. I thought our relationship was different and special. But what could I do? I couldn't push; I would have forced you away. Living a state apart, the plan was that we wouldn't communicate for a week. No seeing each other, no phone calls, no mail. Nothing had precipitated this except perhaps the pace of our relationship. Two decades later, I can see the wisdom of your view and that of other couples who have felt the need for such a time of reflection, but back then I was devastated.

Soon the irritation at this "game" gave way to despair. Perfecting the art of self-doubt, I simply knew beyond certainty that with just a little time away from me, you would see the error of ever considering me. You would realize you could do so much better, and I would get one of those letters or calls that insists we can still be friends.

I didn't realize you were simply testing yourself. You were going to run the possibilities through your mental grid, and once you were satisfied that we were on the right course, you would never doubt or even question the relationship again. That has lasted all these years, and so I'm resignedly glad for the brief period that was so difficult for me.

Something else good came of it, too. I was so miserable and despairing that I was in the pits. I could concentrate on nothing else. Everything in my life suffered during those few days. I ran the thing over and over in my mind so many times that eventually, for my sanity, all I could do was give it to God. And He gave me an insight that was hard to swallow but with which I couldn't argue.

You see, I knew for certain that I could never love anyone else the way I loved you. Had I lost you, I likely would have been a basket case, unable to consider another relationship for a long time. But the Lord seemed to impress upon me that if I truly loved you, I would want the best for you, *even if the best was not me.*

That was a tough one. I didn't want to admit the logic of that, because to me that would be compromising, conceding, giving up. I was already convinced you were going to come to that conclusion, and if I somehow gave even mental assent that I might not be God's perfect will for you, I was doubly sure to lose you.

That made me rethink true love. Did I really love you and want the best for you regardless? Or did I want the best for you only if it included me? How could anyone else be better for you than the person with an infinitely unlimited capacity to love you?

After three days of struggling with that, I gave in. I told God I would accept His, and your, decision, but I pleaded with Him to somehow make it so that if you came to that conclusion, it would be from Him. I didn't want to lose you based on a mistaken judgment call on your part. Big of me, wasn't it?

The next day, I came home from another unproductive day at work to discover that you had called and left a message. After only four days? That could only be bad news! I didn't want to call back. I wasn't ready for the ultimate brush-off of my life.

And yet my curiosity won out. Good or bad, I had to know. I had truly come to terms with God's logic on true love, like it or not. So I called.

You sounded so normal, so like yourself. But then, I had been wise enough to not let you in on my grief. Had I called you a day or so after the hiatus began and sobbed that I couldn't stand this, you would have seen the whimpering wimp I had become and no doubt would have quickly lost interest. It's one thing to be loved. It's another for someone to say, "I'm willing to crawl around in front of you the rest of your life, licking up any dirt you might walk in." What an attractive lover that would make!

You were at first cordial and matter of fact. I, of course, thought you were building to the bad news. Finally you said, "I just wanted to tell you that I think we've had enough time apart. I miss you, and I want to see you. . . . Hello?"

I was nearly speechless. So this abbreviated break had been as much God's way of teaching me something as it was for you to get your mind around the concept of our life together. It was one of the hardest lessons I have ever learned, but I learned it well.

Of course I wanted to see you right away, but my car was laid up. In my youth and foolishness, I asked a friend if I could borrow his car to make a two-hour, one-way drive to see you for an hour before driving back. He had heard just about enough about you and agreed to let me use it if he and his fiancée could come along and meet you. That was one of those crazy trips I'll never forget, but it was worth every minute and every mile.

For better or for worse. Or, as some like to recite it these days, in good times and bad. It takes little commitment to hang together during the good times. This pledge is all about the worse, the bad.

We had few bad times during the first couple of years of marriage. I remember, however, that you were wounded when we showed a close friend the home we intended to buy and he made a disparaging comment about it. It didn't seem that big a deal to me. It certainly doesn't rank with losing a child or another loved one.

And yet I learned about you in your reaction to that. It came up again years later when we were struggling to sell a home. We were weeks past our comfort zone and worrying about two mortgages and all the other turmoil that comes when you can't sell a home when you need to.

The pressure built, and one day a couple came with a Realtor but left after looking at just a room or two. That was almost too much for you. You thought it was rude, but worse, you took it personally. I recall trying to say, "Hey, if they knew it wasn't for them, they didn't need to waste any more time."

But I started to see how close to your heart your home was. It reflected you. In many ways, it *was* you. It reminded me of the time our sump pump went out and we discovered two feet of water in the basement. For some reason, I was strangely calm. It was the first time such a catastrophe was my responsibility. You sat on the steps in tears, maybe from shock more than from loss (we didn't have much to lose), while I foolishly waded through the water to give the pump a nudge. It kicked on and drained that basement in no time, but a plumber later told me I could just as easily have been electrocuted.

Those weren't tragedies. They were learning experiences. It was a privilege for me to stand with you in times of obvious personal stress. But I wondered then, as I do now, when the real "worse" might come. It seems to come to all, but we've been largely spared.

Even the scariest time we spent together—when you were in labor 18 hours with our first and I was light-headed and weak-kneed from excitement and from the distress of seeing you in real pain for the first time—resulted only in glorious happiness.

When you nearly severed a fingertip in a slamming window, I wished it had been me. It was an emergency, a scare, with lots of things to take care of and think about before, during, and after rushing you to the emergency room. Your resilience and strength carried us through that, too. Except for using adrenalin to dislodge that heavy, old window to free you, I didn't even get to be heroic.

Our other "worse" times over the years have come in the form of water problems, building problems, church conflicts, and school-board fights. Those all seem minor in retrospect, and again, compared to real tragedy and grief, they *were* minor. But at the time, they were significant. They caused strife and turmoil, and they divided us from friends. They never came between us, however.

That has been a powerful life's elixir for me—to know we can weather storms. We've traveled together, sometimes in conditions less than ideal. We've worked and ministered and survived together when we were tired, hungry, and frustrated. Never once in all our years together has the thought of divorce entered my mind, and you've told me the same.

Splitting, leaving, abandoning, breaking the vow, is not part of our picture. Admittedly, we may naturally get along better than most couples—at least better than some we know. Struggles, lightweight as they've seemed, tend to draw us closer rather than pull us apart.

We don't agree on everything. That would be boring. But if we have a significant disagreement over something important—a decision about one of the kids, a career or financial choice—we're not worried or intimidated by the initial lack of consensus. We know it will come because we have pledged to stay with each other and love each other for richer, for poorer, for better, for worse.

We sometimes embrace disagreement, never digging in our heels and folding our arms or turning our backs. We listen, and we plead our cases. Sometimes we concede even when we still disagree. And then comes the inevitable moment when one of us obviously has to be proved right. It's amazing how often over the years it has proved correct for one of us to decide reluctantly to give in. Somehow we have a sixth sense, apparently, that tells us when the other is right.

Most gratifying is the fact that the one who was right all along resists the I-told-you-so temptation. We both give input, we see how quickly we can come to agreement, or at least to a decision, and then we're in it together from that point on, regardless of the outcome.

I'm grateful beyond words that this part of our vows has been tested so easily over the years. I'm also encouraged that the early signs show that perhaps those rehearsals have built a little muscle so that when the dire times come, as they're sure to do, we'll be able to stand.

Together.

In love.

Keeping our promises to each other.

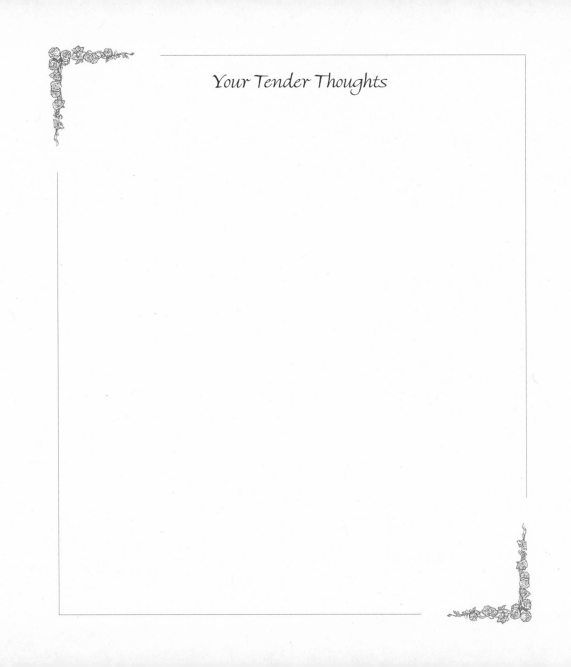

Your Tender Thoughts

For as Long as We Both Shall Live...

For some reason, probably because of the phrase that traditionally precedes it, this has become my favorite part of the wedding vows. That antecedent phrase is, "I will keep you only unto me . . ." Then comes "for as long as we both shall live," which is a modern, more positive substitute for the old "until death us do part."

What a wonderful pledge! I will keep you only unto me for as long as we both shall live. In this day of open marriages and liberal views of vows, we hear of couples opting against saying things like "love, honor, and obey." And worse, we hear them bastardizing this phrase to say "for as long as we both shall *love*."

How convenient! If we fall out of love, all bets are off. Time out! Do over!

When I was a kid, we played marbles with a great rule like that. Before you made your toss, you could say, "Overs!" That meant this was a practice roll, and the only bad part was if you shot your marble right into the hole. You had called overs, so you had to do it over, regardless.

One day a newcomer showed up with a new rule. He called out, "Overs if I need 'em!" Imagine! He could have kept shooting all day! If he missed, he had overs. If he made it, he didn't need them. We laughed him off the playground. We should do that to modern couples who promise to stay with each other, and even to keep themselves only to each other, for as long as they both shall love. Ridiculous!

Breaking down the complete vow phrase by phrase makes it really come alive. "I will keep you . . ." Young, in love, looking at the seemingly limitless future, we have made our choices. Everything I am and all I have, everything I will be and all I will have, will keep (maintain, protect, possess, love, honor, and cherish) everything you are and have and all you will ever be and have.

That's a vow to study. So many young people don't stop and think about what they're saying. The language is too archaic or the pledges are swept past too quickly in a ceremonial ritual that's simply a means to an end. Before God, man, the state, and each other, we're making solemn, legal, sacred promises. I will keep you, and the next word is the operative word in the sentence and an oath that should ring through the ages—*only*.

That's exclusivity. I will keep you only. No one else. And where will I keep you? Unto me. I will keep you only unto me. Need someone be frank and graphic? Have we come to the point where a minister needs to interrupt and ask the couple if they fully understand what they're saying? Wouldn't you love it if he said, "Excuse me, but just so we're all reading from the same page, may I clarify? You just said to your intended, 'I will keep you only unto me.' Do you know what that means?

"Do you understand that the emphasis is not on 'only unto me' but on 'you only'? Keeping another only unto you means he or she will be the only person you will sleep with, make love to, enjoy sex with. That's what it means. To say you will keep someone only unto you means, 'You are the only person in the world I will have sex with for as long as both of us are alive.' "

Sadly, the day may have already come when we need someone to break in and make so plain and pedestrian that beautiful phrase. That vow is being broken every day, and even more sadly, it's being violated by nearly as high a percentage of professing Christians as by others.

What are we *not* saying in that vow? We're not saying that no other person will ever be attractive to us. We're not saying that, though we're thrilled with our choice, we'll never see another person anywhere anytime who is better looking.

How I would like to think that you find me more attractive physically than any other person you will ever see! But I have eyes. I have a mirror. I'm not being falsely modest or begging for compliments. If you married someone 20 times more attractive than me, there would still be someone somewhere who would be more dramatic, sexy, alluring, and exciting.

Too many people, especially men, think that when they marry, they suddenly begin wearing blinders. Before marriage, men seem "polyerotic," as a psychologist has so aptly put it. They can be sexually aroused by any woman, even—and sometimes especially—by ones they don't know. What makes them think that will suddenly change after marriage?

It can be surprising and disappointing to find that lust is still an issue, that appreciating beauty, even in other women, is still going to happen. It needn't be such a trauma. If they're lusting and indulging in inappropriate thoughts or looks, of course those must be dealt with. But spouses aren't vowing to be dishonest. We're not promising that we've been supernaturally reengineered so that no one else looks good to us.

I like to believe you may be the most beautiful woman I've ever seen. You scoff at that, not out of modesty or low self-esteem, but out of your bedrock practicality. Sometimes you even show me pictures of famous lovelies and insist that *there* is real beauty.

And I have to admit that as we both age—as disgusted as both of us are by this society's worship of youth—time and gravity do take their toll (more on me than you—curses!), and we can't really compete with those who were born half our lives ago.

So if we can stipulate, in spite of the fact that our love makes us find each other even more attractive than we are, that there are, indeed, many better-looking people of both sexes in the world, we can put the issue to rest. Because this vow is not a pledge to pretend. We said we would keep each other exclusively unto ourselves for as long as we both shall live. We didn't say we would do this for as long as we were both young, healthy, attractive, and so totally engrossing that no one else would catch our fancy.

For me that's an important distinction, because it takes me out of circulation. There's often a funny scene in romantic comedies where some newlywed catches a glimpse of some eligible single person and wonders or even says aloud—sometimes even to the single person— "What might have happened if I had met you first?"

Do you know that I have never allowed such a thought? It makes no difference. I didn't meet someone else first. I don't care if other women are cuter, prettier, more beautiful, sexier, funnier, more articulate, taller, shorter, heavier, or lighter than you. It's irrelevant.

I don't care that someone else and I might have hit it off better, had more fun talking, had more things in common, made more beautiful music together—whatever. The person who doesn't take to heart this vow of exclusivity could spend the rest of his or her life wondering *What if?*

I'm not looking. I'm not considering. I'm not speculating. I've made my choice, and sticking with it has nothing to do with who else I see or what happens to you. I recall early in our marriage rhapsodizing about your face and your asking me to consider what would happen if it were somehow mutilated. Things happen, you said.

I was stunned by the question, not because I hadn't ever thought of it or considered it, but because of what it revealed about your insecurity—which I suddenly realized I had fed unwittingly. I loved *you*—your character, your inner beauty. Yet I had chosen to compliment the outward appearance. I was probably a victim of societal pressure, assuming that since looks were so important to most, they would be important to you.

There was no question in my mind that if you were in an accident, were burned, or had something else happen that disfigured your face, it would not affect my love for the real you one iota. I understand how some husbands might be embarrassed or feel cheated in that circumstance. But I can't identify with those who would abandon a disfigured wife. I know people do that, and I can think of little more shallow.

Your question taught me a valuable lesson about how I expressed my love, however. I admit I'm enamored with your beauty, and I love to look at you. If something happened that altered your looks, I would miss your attractiveness. But I would still keep you only unto me.

I learned to be clear that your beauty is a bonus. It isn't your looks I'm in love with. It isn't your face to which I made my promises and pledges. It was you.

There's something about the limitation of this exclusivity that's freeing and makes life simpler. Can I say that I've never seen another woman who is fun to look at, talk to, smile at, and be around? No, I can't. But I'm taken. I'm spoken for, and I've spoken for someone else.

The highest honor I can pay to my spoken-for one is to talk about you, to let people know that I'm proud and happy to have made my stand. I show your picture. I don't flirt. I don't touch inappropriately. I've planted hedges around my head, heart, eyes, and hands. I celebrate my wedding anniversary every day.

Just as nothing can separate us from the love of God, neither should anything, save death, separate us from each other. You won't see me turn from you because of illness, poverty, or bad times. You won't hear the excuse that we've grown apart, that we married too young, or that someone else has caught my fancy. Even the most heinous grounds for divorce are also grounds for forgiveness.

Death may not wait for old age. (If it doesn't, it had better hurry!) That's reason enough for us to approach marriage with gusto, enjoying the years together while they last.

The death of a spouse is especially painful because the two have become one flesh. The moment of parting is not unlike the amputation of half our being. Whichever of us remains during that dark hour can find comfort in knowing that a homecoming is not far off that is unlike anything any eye has seen or ear has heard. At that glorious reunion, all tears will be dried, and good-byes will become a thing of the past.

We've both talked about how impossible it seems that either of us would remarry should one of us precede the other in death. My parents feel the same way. My guess is that most happily married people feel that way; that's why their surviving offspring are usually so shocked when they remarry a year or two down the road.

It's hard to imagine developing with someone else the same intimacy, the same oneness, that a lifetime of marriage has afforded us. We hate to think of the surviving spouse in the arms of another. Indeed, many widows and widowers make horrible second-time spouses because they can't lay to rest a lifetime of memories. The new spouse must compete with the most difficult suitor imaginable, the dead mate.

An old joke says that a pastor told his congregation, "If anyone here is perfect, stand to your feet." A man stood. "Charlie," the pastor said, flabbergasted, "are you telling us you're perfect?"

"No, sir," Charlie said. "I'm standing for my wife's first husband."

I can't imagine the emptiness, the aching grief, the remorse, the valley through which I would have to walk if I lost you to death. The idea of one day finding a new love and marrying her hits me like a desecration of your memory. And yet many twice-married people say it doesn't have to be that way. Their spouses understand that the first marriage was wonderful and that the dear departed was a tremendous person.

Some experts suggest a second marriage should be seen as a compliment to the late spouse, an indication that the survivor so loved his or her first marriage that he or she wants to be married again.

As I say, it's still hard to imagine it. But to my way of thinking, a person should never rule out remarriage after the death of a spouse. Some people threaten to haunt their spouses if they remarry. Others promise they won't remarry, then feel terribly guilty when they do.

I can imagine being just as jealous of your new husband if I preceded you in death as I would be if I lost you to another now. And yet what is true love? Remember, I learned it the hard way. I want what's best for you—God's best—even if that's not me.

So while you say you would never remarry—that you can't imagine anyone else being so right for you, anyone loving you the way I do, or you loving another the way you do me—I have to say I wouldn't begrudge it. Depending on your age and our kids' ages, your financial status, and your loneliness, why shouldn't you be happy and have companionship? I wouldn't consider it a desecration or a lack of respect for me or my memory. (And I promise not to haunt you, provided you don't remarry right away!)

They say that men who lose their wives replace them right away, while women who lose their husbands grieve. My guess is that because of the beauty of our relationship, both of us would fall into the latter category.

I prefer to emphasize the first part of this beautiful vow, however. We can worry about the other eventualities if tragedy strikes either of us. Meanwhile, for as long as we both shall live, I will happily keep you only unto me.

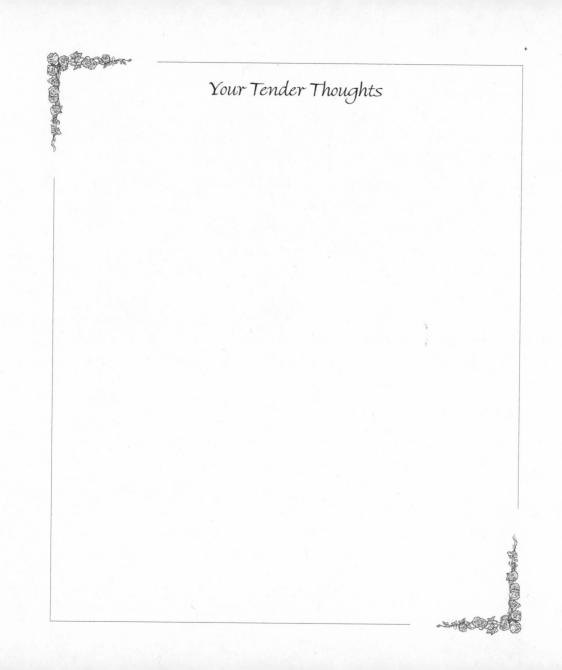

Your Tender Thoughts

With This Ring, I Thee Wed...

*I*f only there were a way for a man to know a woman's ring size without tipping her off that he's about to pop the question! I always wondered how they did it in the old movies. The guy would take his sweetheart to a beautiful, moonlit spot overlooking the twinkling lights of a city. He would begin a vague, rambling conversation about the future, get a few assurances from her that she would love to spend it with him, and then reach into his pocket and produce that tiny box with the most beautiful diamond ring she had ever seen. It would fit perfectly.

In real life, of course, most couples talk about marriage long before they get serious about an official engagement. Sometimes they even talk about the ring and how *they* will afford it. To me, sharing the cost of the ring takes the romance out of it, but even we had to shop so I would know what you liked and what size you wore.

I would have liked to have had a ring in my pocket the night I asked you to share all your tomorrows with me. The problem was, the timing sneaked up even on me. I knew where we were headed, obviously, but I was overcome by the moment and abandoned my plans to ask at a different place and a different time. When it happens and the answer is yes, hindsight always shows everything was perfect.

I was a person of modest means, but I certainly didn't want you sharing in the cost of your own ring. I had to borrow to get for you what I wanted you to have, but I didn't want to drag that debt into our marriage. Maybe my purchase was a tad outlandish for my station in life, but I wanted to avoid the typical reaction when people looked at the engagement ring; there was always some smart guy who would pretend to haul out a magnifying glass to find the tiny stone.

Clearly, the diamond engagement ring is not the ring spoken of in this part of the wedding vow, but there's no mystery why the two tokens are similar. Like the sacrament of baptism, only continually visible, a ring is an outward display of an inner commitment. When we shopped for our wedding rings, we wanted them to be precious gifts to express our commitment to a lifelong bond.

We found matching rings of interlocking carvings that were popular back then, but we both have since lost those rings. Your original diamond disappeared at one point as well—we suspect in a bowl of hamburger you kneaded by hand. (Someone likely downed a very expensive sandwich that day.)

We replaced those losses almost instantaneously, because we felt nearly naked without our rings. They mean so much, signify so much, are so special to us. When we're apart, they represent us to each other and remind us of our commitments. They also show the world that we're taken.

You've often expressed irritation with men you know who are married but don't wear wedding rings. They may have valid reasons, but I agree that even a bit of discomfort is worth a spouse's peace of mind. (Of course, there are a few exceptions, like working with certain kinds of machinery, where wearing any kind of ring would be dangerous.) I proudly wear my ring. The old joke says that what a

wedding ring and a rubber band on the finger have in common is
that both cut off your circulation.

Much is made in modern wedding ceremonies of the fact that the
ring is an unbroken circle, a symbol of eternal love. It should also
represent the truth that we will one day be joined forever with our
heavenly Bridegroom.

This comparison of human marriage to the biblical picture of the
church as Christ's perfect bride is beautiful and intimidating. It has
always been difficult for me to live under the injunction from the
apostle Paul about husbands loving their wives as Christ loved the
church and gave Himself for it. But how must it be for wives to live
up to the standard of being spotless, perfect, as pure as the bride of
Christ?[1]

We do better when we enjoy the imagery and the promises of the
infinite, eternal, perfect One who loves us. Only He can live up to
those ideals. They're pictures, examples, goals for us to shoot for, real-
izing that in our human weakness we must rely on Him to live out
such ideals through us.

I learned a hard lesson as a child about loving anyone enough to
be willing to lay down my life for him. I was the third of three sons. I
enjoyed being the baby of the family, but only to a point. When I

reached eight or nine years old, I began praying for a baby brother or sister. I'll never forget the night at the dinner table a year or so later when my dad asked us boys what one thing we would want if we could have anything in the world. (He enjoyed such games, such dramatic announcements.)

Despite my prayers, I wasn't thinking about a baby just then. I probably thought of things I'd like to have, places I'd like to go, things I'd like to become. My brothers responded the same way. But when Dad started probing, asking me what I had been praying for, it hit me all of a sudden. He was trying to tell us something.

We were so excited about the impending child that we were nearly speechless. Then we began jumping around and singing, "We're gonna have a baby!"

When Jay came along, ten years after the rest of us, he was the hit of the family. I was especially close to him, always taking him places, showing him off, taking care of him. When he became a toddler, I took him with me when we went to the store, holding his hand as we crossed the streets.

Then one day the whole family was walking back from a swimming pool, and Jay and I were at a corner half a block ahead. He had been walking with me, not holding my hand but staying close. The light changed, and we walked across a busy intersection. When I reached the other side, I turned to see that for some reason, Jay had stopped in the middle of the crosswalk. Just then the light changed, and the traffic began moving around him.

I froze. At 13, with my three-year-old brother in mortal danger in the middle of the street, I'd like to think I'd have been heroic, dodging traffic and racing to save him. But I wasn't. I just stood there as my mother came running, having seen the whole thing unfold.

She ignored the traffic and darted into the street to scoop him up and rush him to where I stood. She didn't have to scold me or even give me a look, though I'll never forget her face that day. To her credit, she didn't punish me or try to make me feel bad. She knew how I felt.

A year or so later, in a class assignment in high school, we were asked to write on a slip of paper the one person in the world we would die for. Classmates wrote things like their mother, their father, their boyfriend, their best friend, their brother or sister. I wrote, "No one."

I knew that if I wasn't able to risk my life for the brother for whom I had prayed for years, I wasn't ready to die for anyone. The teacher looked up from reading the results and said, "Well, there's one honest person in this class."

I don't know if it was honesty or a certain gritty maturity born of a bad experience. More than 30 years later, I'd like to think I've grown to the point where I would have the courage to do the right thing. There are many people in my life I would hope to be willing to die for: you, our sons, my parents. I make no rash predictions or promises, because that old memory is still fresh and painful, but, as I say, I'd like to think . . .

Ominous to me is that the Scriptures I purport to set my course by make it an injunction that I'm to love my wife as Christ loved the church and was willing to die for her. No mere sentiment, this is a command. This is what I'm supposed to do. I'm willing; that's all I can say. My ring is symbolic of all the commitments I made the day we were married.

My father, your father-in-law, is one of the most romantic men I've ever known. He has always been a man's man, an ex-Marine and a retired police chief; yet he's also a poet and tender of heart. He has been so devoted to my mother for so many years that their relation-ship fills my memory banks.

Five years before I was born, a year before they were married, they were in the midst of a 33-month absence from each other. Dad and Mom were engaged as teenagers, and then he went off to fight in World War II. Those were difficult, terror-filled days.

All around him, the others in his outfit received Dear John letters. One by one, their sweethearts found someone else and wrote to deliver the bad news. Dad saw each man's confidence ebb away as the sickle of disappointment struck down one and then another. Yet he remained confident of my mother's true love. They wrote nearly every day, but because of the distance and the situation, some letters took weeks to arrive.

It was one thing to wonder if you would be alive the next day. It was another to wonder whether your lover would still love you and wait for you. In the middle of all that, Dad wrote poems to the girl waiting for him at home. I offer here three of my favorites that may reveal where some of my romanticism and—who knows?—my predilection for writing came from.[2]

Meditation
by Harry P. Jenkins
October 1944

Shades of night, so fast are falling,
Ending one more lonely day;

Makes me one day nearer to you,
Yet you're still so far away.

Days are long and hot and dreary,
Nights are short and restless too;
Seems my only consolation
Is in thoughts and dreams of you.

Memories clear, though far behind us,
Still shed light upon the way;
Renew a faith in one another,
Give new meaning to a day.

As the clock counts out the hours,
And the sunset ends a day;
As a full moon starts a new month,
So it prompts me here to say,

"I could never love another,
As I truly do love you;
And I'm living, praying, longing,
For the day our dreams come true."

May We Not Love
by Harry P. Jenkins
October 1944

May we not love though cannons roar;
May we not love though we may die;
That in the battle's darkest hour,
Memories dear might light our sky.

May we not have our private lives;
May we not each our castles build;
That we might hold a world of peace
Where wants and needs might both be filled.

With memories of your fond embrace,
The warming touch of velvet hands,
Can I escape the love you gave
E'en though I travel foreign lands?

To love is life—as we have loved;
Without your love, my life is vain.

Our plans must grow though we must part,
For someday we'll be one again.

I include this last one, my favorite of the many hundreds of poems my dad has written over the years, because it perfectly expresses how I feel about the ring, the theme of this chapter.

The Yellow Band of Gold
by Harry P. Jenkins
November 1944

When lovers part for e'en a day—
For worthy cause or no,
An empty heart must stay behind,
An empty heart must go.

The emptiness is still and dull—
Good times and smiles are few;
Unless a letter, two or three,
Will change the gray to blue.

The daily letter does the trick—
But lest a line grow old,
Rely upon a sterner stuff,
A yellow band of gold.

That yellow band will light the way
In lovelife's darkest hour,
Renews a smile—relives a kiss,
Gives courage with new power.

This seal of gold will say, "He's mine.
He's mine and I am his."
Those words will echo in his heart,
No matter where he is.

Perhaps he's in a foreign land—
Or far out on the blue;
His deepest meditations are
His thoughts of love for you.

What is this yellow band of gold?
Is it a wedding ring?

With This Ring, I Thee Wed...

Is it a picture or a watch?
Or is it everything?

To me the seal is everything
That I am fighting for;
Yes, it's a ring and it's a watch
But yet it's something more.

It seals a vow made long ago—
It's filed in realms above;
In truth, it is a gift from God,
This band—the seal of love.

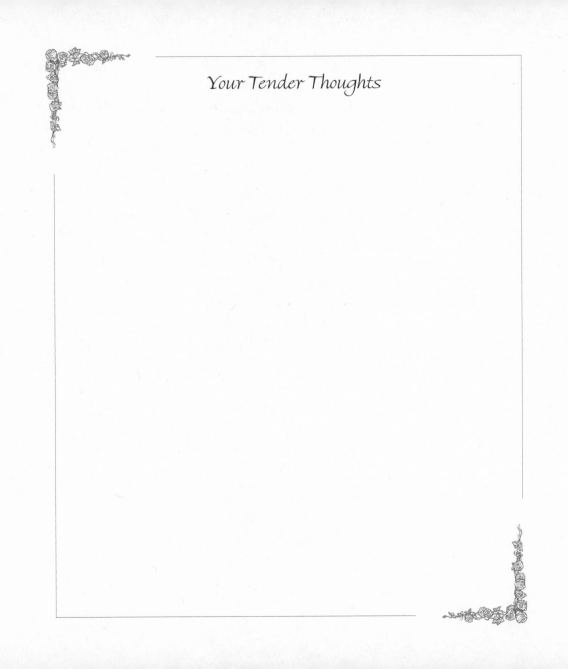

Your Tender Thoughts

You May Kiss...

T he first wedding I recall took place when I was six or seven years old. My mother remembers my being concerned about the ushers leading to their seats some of the women I knew to be married. "What's she doing, taking his arm?" I demanded.

From somewhere, I already had embedded in my brain and heart the idea that marriage was exclusive. One man for one woman, loyal, faithful to the end. Back then, unrelated people of opposite sexes generally didn't touch each other except to shake hands. Women might embrace each other, but even in church you just didn't see the kind of hugging between unrelated men and women that we see today.

While I'm cautious about such embraces, I've come to believe that we are largely healthier as a Christian community because we now allow such brotherly and sisterly physical interaction. People need to be touched—appropriately, of course. Yet with this new freedom have also come some high costs. Men can enjoy embracing other women for reasons less noble than the women might have for enjoying the embrace. (Some women may be less than noble in their interest in this as well, though I hesitate to speak for them.)

I couldn't count the number of weddings I've attended since childhood. I've seen all manner of friends and relatives marry, and I love the pageant. Most of the weddings I've attended have been traditional and formal, but I've also seen a few where different things were tried. They all come down to this, though: The minister tells the bridegroom that he may kiss the bride.

I'm an easy mark for the emotionalism of weddings. It makes a difference how closely related to or how much a friend I am of the people being wed, but even at the wedding of an acquaintance, I can be moved nearly to tears by the expressions of love and commitment.

Seeing the parents of the wedding party in tears makes it difficult for me to remain dry eyed. And since our marriage, I've always accepted the minister's challenge and renewed my vows silently while sitting with you.

I almost chuckle when they get to this last part, though. "You may kiss the bride"? As if the bridegroom needs the minister's permission! Yet there's something much deeper and more symbolic happening here. The minister is speaking for God, for the state, and even for the assembled guests as he leads the way through the pomp and circumstance.

What he's saying at this point is that all the prerequisites have been fulfilled. The statements have been made, the promises and rings have been exchanged, and the matter has been settled legally, sacredly, and morally. He has pronounced the couple man and wife, and now the bridegroom may kiss the bride.

This is their first kiss as man and wife.

I've heard stories of people who literally have not kissed until they were married. I doubt I've ever attended the wedding of such a couple. There are still those, however, who teach that that's the only moral and proper thing to do.

There's a certain quaintness and purity to that, but in my mind it calls for an awfully short courtship and engagement. Waiting to consummate our marriage was difficult enough for me without having to wait to even kiss you.

In this age, it's becoming more and more rare that couples—even Christians—remain sexually pure before marriage. Only a fool would not understand the pressure and the temptation. Sexuality is progressive. Any married couple can remember when they met. Maybe they didn't even like each other at first. Their progression to marriage and sexuality took the long route.

You and I met on a blind date, and I think it's safe to say there were no immediate sparks. But as in any relationship that becomes love, engagement, and marriage, at some point the progression began. There's initial attraction, growing chemistry and familiarity, and then there's touching. It may take the form of sitting close, touching an arm while talking, eventually holding hands, then embracing.

What's more exciting and fun than the pure expressions of deepening affection toward one whom we may marry? I had been engaged in the past, and though I hadn't dated for about a year when I met you, I was grateful that I didn't have regrets or things from that relationship that I needed to keep hidden.

You had dated but had never been in love, and I was thrilled that your "experience" was even more limited than mine. I would have hated to have had to confess to you inappropriate actions, even things far short of having sex, which I wanted to save for marriage. To have had to hear such things from you would have been devastating as well.

What those stages of intimacy are vary with every couple. It's important at some point in a serious relationship to talk frankly about them. If one of the two believes that even deep kissing is something he or she would not want to do before marriage, obviously the other needs to know that. The Scriptures are clear that sexual intercourse before marriage is sin. They're not specific about the many stages of foreplay, but plainly, counselors can tell you that many a remorseful couple approaches their honeymoon as virgins only in a technical sense. In other words, they have done virtually "everything but . . ."

Maybe during my first engagement I had deep in the back of my mind the knowledge, or at least the intuition, that the relationship might not work out. Despite the length of the relationship and the inevitability of physiological progression, we were chaste and careful. This was a virtuous woman I thought I would marry, and both of us were strong when we needed to be, because we didn't want to be impure at our wedding, whether we married each other or someone else.

That's a good thing for young people to think about. They should want to do a favor to their loved one's future spouse, even and especially if they are that future spouse. I'm gratified and proud—in the right sense—that my first fiancée was able to marry without regrets, secrets, or confessions that could have caused her husband mental anguish. And had *I* married her, I would have known she was pure.

When my relationship with you progressed from looks and smiles to holding hands, embracing, and kissing, it was right, appropriate, and wonderful. We weren't unaware of the progressive nature of it. That's why I think the apostle Paul advised people to marry rather than to burn with lust. On the one hand, we encourage long-enough engagements so that the couple can be sure—a broken engagement is much less painful and chaotic than a broken marriage. But on the other hand, we discourage unnecessarily long engagements because the sexual tension and pressure may begin to dominate the relationship.

This happens all the time. A couple hits it off and falls in love, and they seem to talk for hours. They learn everything they can about each other and enjoy laughing, discussing, arguing, and making up, all the while basically becoming an embryonic pair. But when their physical relationship progresses to where all they can think about is consummating their love, they wind up—to be blunt—making out more and talking less.

In many cases, a couple goes from 100 miles an hour of really getting to know each other's minds and hearts to 1,000 miles an hour of getting to know each other's bodies. And then what happens to the really important stuff, the learning of the real character? That had been happening for a while, and they became satisfied that what they had learned was good enough to proceed headlong into marriage. The Christian couple, the ones who care about purity and virginity, then spend most of their time on a precipice. They play around the edges of sin, justifying getting closer and closer to intercourse because they "just know" they're going to be married.

Only someone who has been married for years can look back with the perspective of time and try to point out the proper place the sexual life takes in a marriage. But two people who haven't been there yet aren't listening anyway. I could wave a bony finger at young people and say, "Someday you'll know. Yes, the physical relationship is important and beautiful, but eventually it will take a backseat to the really crucial stuff." But they're not buying. And I wasn't either at that age.

The physical relationship is still thrilling and beautiful, and couples who remain emotionally, mentally, and spiritually close will see their sexual life becoming all the better with the years. But when you've been through the ups and downs of careers, churches, children, schools, and finances, you soon discover what's really important in a relationship.

The minister at our wedding said something that day that I still remember. He said that even if he had gotten a raise, hit a home run in the church softball game, and been told by the elders that they wanted him to spend his next 30 years in that church, he would be miserable if he was out of sorts with his wife. If, however, his paycheck bounced, he struck out in a crucial situation, and the elders told him he needed more schooling, everything would still be fine if his wife smiled at him when he got home.

How true that lesson has become over the years! I feel I can handle whatever life throws my way as long as you're standing with me, loving me, supporting me. But if I landed the best deal an author could dream of and made a fortune on a best-seller, it would mean nothing if we were unhappy with each other.

When I was told that I might kiss my bride, I gave to you with that kiss all that I've ever been or will be, exclusively. The promises I had just made, my whole future, and all my energies were sealed in that moment, and I dedicated myself to making and keeping you happy.

That's a vulnerable spot to be in, because a demanding, childish spouse could take advantage of such love and commitment. Because of our devotion to each other, either of us could have made life miserable for the other by pouting until he or she was satisfied in every situation. Yet our personalities are such that we compete to see who can be the first to clear the air when necessary. I want us always to run into each other trying to outgive and outcompromise.

We're supposed to prefer the other over ourselves. That goes against human nature, and I can't say for a moment that I'm not selfish and wouldn't love to be served and have the world revolve around me. But you've been an example. And when you defer and prefer and do things you know will make me happy, it makes me want to do the same for you.

Sometimes it's hard for us to make a decision because we're both maneuvering to be sure we're doing what the other would like.

"No, really, whatever you want."

"No, you decide."

"I really don't care. Suit yourself."

"If you're happy, I'm happy."

That can get to be a frustrating comedy of errors, but it's sure a better problem than you often hear of, when people get into shouting matches along the lines of "We always do what you want to do! What about me?"

Our first official kiss as husband and wife started us on the road to honoring each other over ourselves. Kissing is still fun, exciting, dramatic, a rush, a promise, exclusive, and sacred. It means so much more today than it did even on the day we were married. That's why I've counseled our kids and any other young person who cares to listen, "Don't lightly give or take a kiss, regardless of the emotion of the moment. Make it solemn; make it mean something."

I'm not so naive as to think that the typical couple doesn't kiss until their wedding day; neither do I think it's unusual for bride and bridegroom to have kissed several others in the past. But when that minister says you may kiss, meaning for the first time as husband and wife, it should signal a lifetime of fidelity and faithfulness that will make the entire scope of married life the focus of your being for as long as you both shall live.

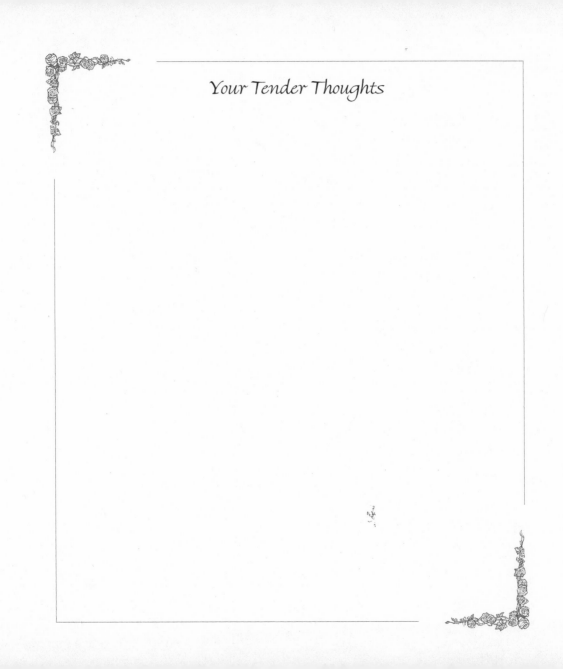

Your Tender Thoughts

I Now Present Mr. and Mrs. ...

Nature's splashes of color are in themselves proof that pleasure is one of God's high priorities. Nothing compares with the delights He has reserved for us in our embrace of love. What has begun at the wedding ceremony as a symbolic kiss is soon consummated in passion so all-consuming that we can only thank God for His pleasurable design.

We have been presented to the assembled, and thus to society, as a new unit, husband and wife, Mr. and Mrs., one in Christ, soon to become one flesh. Passion, like the hormones that fuel it, can be skittish. It can vanish with an unkind word, a cold glance, even a minor irritation.

But when the urges disappear, I won't panic and seek my youth or the reassurance that I'm still a viable human being by looking for someone else. The same passion that drew me to you, if not properly channeled, could wreck our marriage and destroy our legacy.

When passion ebbs, we have never run home to Mother or even slept in separate beds. Often, making up is all it takes to reignite the fire. One of the great delights of my life is that we've never had an extended period of coolness toward each other. (I realize many couples haven't been so fortunate.) Of course, there have been slights, shortness, and disagreements. But we don't raise our voices or say things we have to take back later, for they can't really be taken back, can they?

Often one spouse will scream at the other, "I wish I had never married you!" "I want a divorce!" "My mother was right about you!" or "I hate you!" Then, an hour or a day later, the one who made the ugly remark has to say, "I take it back. I didn't mean it."

I'm grateful we've never traded such mean-spirited barbs, for there is no retrieving them. There's forgiveness, sure, but forgetting such a remark calls for a measure of the divine that we won't enjoy until heaven.

Early in our marriage you said something bordering on sarcasm, and I think I scared you by reacting quickly. I said, "Please don't start down that road. I was raised with three brothers, and I just know that sarcasm is a sport I'm too good at. I would win, you would be hurt, and it would be no fun for either of us."

You said simply, "Okay," and for more than two decades I haven't heard a word of sarcasm from you, nor have you from me. We come to each other straight up and directly when we're hurt, when we feel slighted, insulted, or disappointed. We work quickly not to smooth it over or sweep it under the rug, but to deal with whatever is the problem. What a joy to be able to say that the healthiest relationship I've ever had with anybody has been with you, the most important person in my life! Believe me, I know how unique that is and how many married couples long to return to the idyllic, seemingly idealistic relationship they once enjoyed.

That doesn't mean we always tell each other the whole truth. That sounds heretical to some, but we've learned by experience that our way is better than airing every grievance. We both know that the other has idiosyncrasies and foibles that might be irritating. But we decide carefully whether dealing with them is worth the fallout. What would be the point of making an issue of them? When I'm not all that you wish I would be, you seldom make me feel small. It's just your dumb husband who can do some things swimmingly and can be an airhead about others.

We'll tell each other if something we're wearing doesn't look the best, but if it's not a major issue, we roll with it. Brutally honest spouses tend to nag, to speak their minds about everything, to criticize, correct, and force the other into their mold. We strive to allow ourselves to be individuals, to permit each other to wear our hair the way we like it, even if the other has another preference. Our philosophy is, "If you like it and feel good that way, that's the way you should wear it."

We also try to avoid using words like *never* and *always*. Our goal is to be kind to one another, preferring one another over ourselves and treating each other the way we would treat a guest in our home. That's not easy. How often have you seen a parent go from an argument with a spouse or yelling at a child to picking up a ringing phone with the kindest, gentlest, most heartwarming tone of voice? Some people say they wish their spouses would speak to them as lovingly as they do to the dog or cat.

You have modeled manners and politeness, something my mother tried to teach me for years but which was somehow derailed in a household otherwise filled with men. You rarely badger or condescend, and you say "please" and "thank-you" and respond nicely even within the family. I realize how rare that is.

That isn't to say you've never uttered a cross word or lost your temper. But you've often been an example to me of how to treat the people with whom you live.

Of course, our ultimate model is God. Unlike any other relationship, marriage is human love based on the greater love of God. It's scary to think about—and maybe in this area a little intimidation is good—but there are serious consequences if we reflect poorly on God's love. All people should know we're disciples of Christ by how we love each other. That's clear in the Scriptures. If we don't evidence that love in our own marriages, how do we expect to model it in the church or in the marketplace?

People will judge Him by how we treat each other. They'll examine our love and decide whether Jesus is, in fact, the Son of God. When we stood at the altar, evidenced our exclusive choice, and made our sacred, lifetime vows, more than a marriage was being performed. More than two lives were at stake.

We were playing out a pageant. We were engaged in a real-life picture of the divine love of heaven. I don't know what the statistics show regarding how many wedding guests have come to Christ, but God knows. For some people in that audience, eternity hung in the balance.

That's why I become more thankful with each passing year that God led me to you. Whatever part I thought I had played in searching for and finding the right mate I now discount in the light of half a lifetime of marriage. You've been all and more than I could have ever dreamed, and I'm now firmly entrenched in the school of thought that says God ordains these unions from beginning to end.

For a long time, I've encouraged couples to tell each other their stories. Every time they remember aloud how they met, they're actually telling two versions of the same story. They need to be reminded of those days when each unfailingly put his or her best foot forward, and in the process they'll recall what attracted each to the other. They'll also realize anew how clearly God led.

In our case, for instance, how did a guy born in Michigan and raised near Chicago meet in Indiana a girl raised in rural, downstate Illinois? I remember that bleak period between the breakup of my first engagement and the time friends encouraged the two of us to get

together on a blind date. I sat at the kitchen table in my parents'
house, lamenting the fact that "they don't make women like Mom"
anymore. I used to joke that every time I found a girl who could
cook like my mother, she looked like my father—not a politically
correct line nowadays.

I was rehearsing a long list of eligible women I knew, contemplat-
ing aloud whether I might want to ask them out. Several were wonderful people, but I had always been a romantic, looking for a spark,
something special—chemistry. As I talked about each, I was either
not too hopeful or thought of reasons why we would be better
friends than "items." Occasionally I would think of a real possibility,
only to have my mother say, "I heard she's engaged [or married]."

Finally Mom said, "I don't know. I just have a feeling you haven't
yet met the one you're going to marry."

I couldn't imagine that. Would there still be someone unclaimed
for me, someone chaste, virginal, spiritual, wonderful—someone like
that who would want me? It was nice to think about, but it seemed
like a dream.

We were urged to agree reluctantly to a blind date, doubling with
mutual friends. I had seen your picture and was intimidated. I knew
I never would have asked you out on my own. You were out of my

class (may it ever be so). But the word was that everyone was intimidated by your beauty and your height and so you were not as much in demand as one might think. I was surprised. I would have thought you might be able to work me into your schedule in six months.

I also thought blind dates were supposed to be bad news. It's intimidating to realize, when you look in the mirror, that *you're* the bad news. The meeting was awkward, but you were as tall and beautiful in person as you had been in those campus-queen's-court pictures I had seen. Imagine me dating a member of the queen's court! This would be fun while it lasted.

You had a beautiful smile and were friendly and cordial. You also had a sense of ease with a stranger, which I find more puzzling today, because that's not your strength; you have to work at it. You were working hard at it and succeeding that night.

I found you engaging, fun, and pleasant, but no fireworks went off. We saw each other again the next night and began corresponding. I lived near Chicago and you in Fort Wayne, Indiana. After a while, I thought I had at least made a nice friend. I wasn't sure about pursuing anything serious. The friend who introduced us thought I was nuts.

I was.

I arranged a date for just the two of us a few weeks later, worrying that I was implying something I didn't mean to. I didn't want to lead you on, and I didn't think either of us, already in our twenties, was interested in dating someone just for companionship.

But that night, it was love at third sight. I was so overwhelmed that I was speechless. The moment I saw you, I knew more assuredly and clearly than I had ever known anything before that I would be spending the rest of my life with you.

I couldn't tell you, of course. You'd have run from me. I just knew. It wasn't hope or speculation or a dream. I knew absolutely. If it hadn't worked out, I'd still be reeling 20-plus years later.

I didn't know what had happened to me or what had changed. All I knew was that I had been given a glimpse of the future, and we were in it together. When you stood in the kitchen preparing a meal, I knew I would see and help you do this for years to come. When you looked me in the eye and spoke to me, I knew I would be getting used to your melodious voice and that we would communicate just like this all our married lives.

From that moment, I never doubted that we were meant to be together, and I wish I could quantify the reason or get a handle on it somehow. As counsel to young people, it comes off moony, romantic, and mystical. Maybe it wasn't a good basis on which to build a relationship, but I was so sure.

I still am.

I hadn't even held your hand yet, let alone embraced or kissed you. By the end of that evening, however, I couldn't have said the same. We walked in a downpour, and you worried about what was happening to your hair. You looked every bit as beautiful then, soaking wet from head to toe, as you do to me today.

All I wanted to do was touch you, look into your eyes, and talk to you. When we were apart, I wanted to call you, to go and see you. I wrote you often. Our phone bills went sky high. I was gone, head over heels, helpless, hapless.

I took pictures of you, and when I couldn't be with you, I sat at home, projected them on the wall, and gazed at you. Any other relationship I had ever thought was love paled in comparison to this. My parents had once told me, "You'll know. You'll just know."

Maybe they had predisposed me for a time such as this. It showed. I glowed. People would ask me what I was so happy about. I was so proud it showed that I was eager to tell them, to show your picture, to ask if they wanted to see the big one I projected on the wall. (They didn't.)

I was so in love that I didn't even hope you would one day share my enthusiasm. Obviously I prayed you would love me and agree to marry me, but I knew I was so deeply in love that it was too much to ask that my depth of feeling be reciprocated. In all honesty, I didn't feel worthy of the kind of love from you that I felt for you.

You were careful and methodical in your reactions to me. I was careful to not bowl you over and push you away. But when the day came that you decided (based on no prior experience, you said) you loved me, too, it was the highlight of my life. You said something about not being able to otherwise explain your joy when you were with me and your misery when we were apart. "I don't know what else to call it or what else to say," you concluded. "I love you."

"I love you" were the words we each used at the ends of our individual wedding vows. That old song that says "I love you more today than yesterday, but not as much as tomorrow" is no sappy sentiment to me. You're still the one.

With this ring, I thee wed, and I will keep you only unto me for as long as we both shall live.

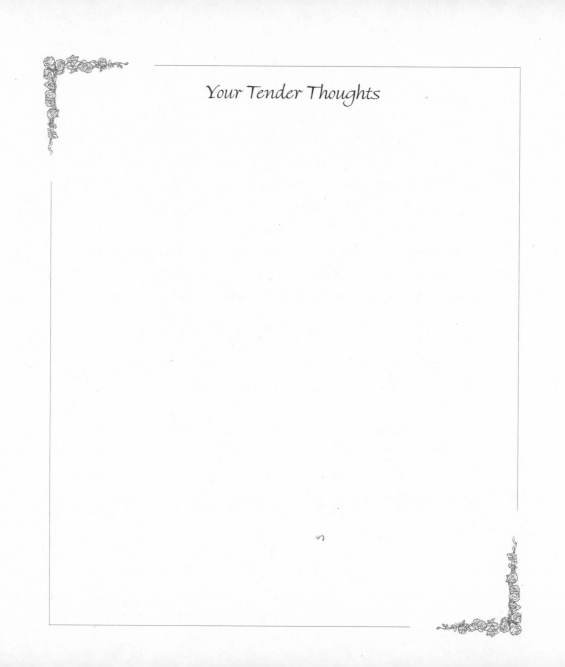

Your Tender Thoughts

Notes

Chapter 3

1. 1 Timothy 4:12.

Chapter 5

1. See James 2:17.
2. See Luke 2:19.

Chapter 6

1. See James 4:14.

Chapter 10

1. See Ephesians 5:25-27.
2. From *Poetry, Jenkins Style/The Poetry of Harry P. Jenkins,* copyright 1991 by Jerry B. Jenkins.